PUFFIN BOOKS

MR BROWSER MEETS THE MIND SHRINKERS

Whoever heard of sweets turning children into robots?

When Mr Smith, a new supply teacher, stands in for Mr Browser at Chivvy Chase School, a sinister plot to take over the world begins – for Mr Smith is a Mind Shrinker. He is very strict with Class 8 and the only good thing about him is that he gives out sweets at the beginning of each lesson – Mind Bogglers, Taste Ticklers, Lips Smackers and – best of all – Telly Mates.

When Spiky Jackson returns to school after a week's holiday in Spain, he finds Class 8 completely under the supply teacher's spell. They're all working hard, all very quiet and not answering back – Spiky knows that something is wrong. Can it be anything to do with the sweets?

Another very funny, and mysterious, story about the pupils of Chivvy Chase School and the lovable teacher Mr Browser.

Philip Curtis started to write when he was given an empty exercise book and stayed home one hot day to fill it up, instead of going swimming. His first 'Mr Browser' book was written from his own experience as a teacher and was published about eighteen months after he'd written it. Philip Curtis lives in Leigh-on-Sea in Essex.

Other books by Philip Curtis

MR BROWSER AND THE BRAIN SHARPENERS
MR BROWSER AND THE SPACE MAGGOTS

Mr Browser Meets the Mind Shrinkers

PHILIP CURTIS

Illustrated by Tony Ross

PUFFIN BOOKS

PUFFIN BOOKS

Published by the Penguin Group
Penguin Books Ltd, 27 Wrights Lane, London W8 5TZ, England
Viking Penguin, a division of Penguin Books USA Inc.
375 Hudson Street, New York, New York 10014, USA
Penguin Books Australia Ltd, Ringwood, Victoria, Australia
Penguin Books Canada Ltd, 2801 John Street, Markham, Ontario, Canada L3R 1B4
Penguin Books (NZ) Ltd, 182–190 Wairau Road, Auckland 10, New Zealand

Penguin Books Ltd, Registered Offices: Harmondsworth, Middlesex, England

First published by Andersen Press Limited 1989
Published in Puffin Books 1991
1 3 5 7 9 10 8 6 4 2

Printed in England by Clays Ltd, St Ives plc

Contents

1	Mr Smith Takes Shape	7
2	Mind Bogglers and Taste Bud Ticklers	9
3	The Mind Shrinkers' Master Plan	30
4	The Return of Spiky Jackson	42
5	The Mr Browser Mystery	58
6	Deadline Monday Morning	85
7	The Mind Shrinkers' Mental Test	100
8	No More Mind Bogglers	115
9	Mr Smith Goes to Pieces	125

1
Mr Smith Takes Shape

When the Mind Shrinkers sent their agent down to earth for the experiment at Chivvy Chase, they naturally chose for him the most common English name they could find—Mr Smith.

His landing place was also carefully chosen. He descended one night from a satellite invisible to human eyes, and landed on a piece of grassland just beyond a sandpit outside the town of Chivvy Chase. Had anyone been around at that time of night they wouldn't have known that Mr Smith was there, for he was beamed down as a collection of cells which lay like soft wax on the ground. Then, under the influence of yellowish rays, the cells showed signs of life, and slowly the form of Mr Smith took shape. Beside him was a plastic covered parcel, and a little further away were several boxes, which lay near a tree which had only a few days before been struck by lightning, set on fire and thus made hollow.

When Mr Smith had taken human shape, he quickly opened the plastic like parcel and brought out a complete set of clothing. He dressed himself, and out of one of the pockets of his jacket took a pair of horn-rimmed type spectacles, which he placed on his nose. Now he looked as smart as any business man, or even a diplomat or politician. He wore a wig of smooth black hair brushed well back, and his eyes twinkled behind the glasses, giving him a slightly owlish appearance. He walked over to the distant boxes, placed several of them inside the hollow tree, throwing them up to the top of the trunk expertly, as though he had been practising this. Then he took the two biggest boxes under his arms and set off in the direction of the town.

The collection of cells known as Mr Smith was now ready for action, and the Chivvy Chase experiment was about to begin.

2

Mind Bogglers and Taste Bud Ticklers

Michael Fairlie arrived in the school playground on the first day after the half-term holiday, looking much happier than he normally did on such occasions. He was wearing a jacket, because the weather was much colder than it ought to be at the end of October, and both his jacket pockets were bulging. He looked around the playground at the different groups of children, hoping to see some of his classmates. Spiky Jackson, he knew, would not be there; Spiky had gone with his parents for a fortnight's holiday to Spain, and so would enjoy an extra week off school.

Anna Cardwell was there amidst a group of six girls, but Michael hurried past them, not because they were girls but because there were too many of them for him to be able to impress them with his news. He had something to tell and something to share with one or two friends—and he didn't want to give everything he had in his pockets away at once. He saw Jason Little and Selwyn Jordan in a corner of the playground, their heads together over a comic, and with a swift, darting run he joined them.

'Hi, Jason, hi, Selwyn!'

'Hello, Mike,' said Jason, without looking away from his comic.

'Is that so interesting?' demanded Michael. 'I've news for you, I think. Which way did you two come to school this morning?'

'The usual way,' said Selwyn, turning over a page of the comic. 'Why?'

'You didn't come along Chase Road?'

'Of course we didn't. Why should we?'

'Then you don't know!'

'Don't know what?' asked Jason, looking at Michael for the first time.

'You remember the paper shop that closed down last year—the one on the corner of Chase Road, where we used to buy ices and sweets?'

'And?' asked Jason coolly.

'Well, it's just reopened. The woman in it said I was one of the first customers. I bought some sweets there, and they're new brands.'

Now the comic was forgotten, and Michael's pockets were the centres of attention.

'Have you ever seen these?' he asked, pulling a bag out of each pocket. 'You can try one of each. They taste pretty good.'

Selwyn took a paper covered sweet from the bag in Michael's left hand, and Jason took an orange coloured one from the other. They inspected the

sweets carefully.

'Taste Bud Ticklers!' said Selwyn. 'I've never heard of them.'

'What about these!' said Jason, laughing. 'Mind Bogglers! What sort of sweet is that?'

'Try them,' suggested Michael, and unwrapped a Mind Boggler himself before returning the bags to his pockets.

For a few seconds they faced one another, lost in silent chewing.

'Not bad,' decided Jason, working the sweet alongside his cheek so that he could speak. 'Mine tastes like a kind of fruity mint. It's really good, Mike!'

'Mine's a kind of chocolate toffee mixture,' declared Selwyn. 'I've never tasted anything like it before!'

'They've several other kinds,' Michael told them. 'And they only cost 30p a bag.'

'I'm going home that way,' said Jason. 'I bet they'll sell like wildfire.'

Michael chewed away contentedly, pleased to have made the effect on them he had hoped to do. He found the taste of the sweets so excellent that it was easy to conquer his desire to tell everybody about them; he realised that if he did so, he would have to give out samples and would be left with hardly any for himself. He was chewing a sweet when he entered school, and Mr Sage, the Headmaster, warned him to be rid of it as soon as possible, so he chewed even faster.

As he sat in the classroom he was more aware of the sweets in his pockets than of the lessons Mr Browser was taking. During maths he popped a Taste Bud Tickler in his mouth, and by frowning over his sums managed to eat it without being caught. When Mr Browser changed to an English lesson, Michael couldn't resist a Mind Boggler—

and this time he wasn't so lucky.

'You've had all the holiday in which to eat sweets, Michael Fairlie,' said Mr Browser. 'Put that out in the basket, and please try and think about the lesson.'

Michael obeyed, but with all good intentions he found he was still concentrating more on the sweets than on his English. At last the bell rang for play, and out in the playground he took out one of the paper bags. Jason and Selwyn were beside him at once.

'Let's have another one, Mike,' pleaded Jason. 'I'll pay you back as soon as I've bought some.'

'So will I,' added Selwyn, who usually showed little interest in sweets. 'Just one, Mike, please.'

As Michael was handing out the sweets, Anna Cardwell ran past and caught a glimpse of the paper bags. She was back in a flash.

'Sweets!' she cried. 'Is it your birthday, Mike?'

'Give her one, Mike,' said Jason. 'See what she thinks of them.'

Michael could see that if he didn't give her one, she would be a nuisance to him perhaps all day long, so he agreed.

'Have a Mind Boggler,' he said, pushing the bag towards her. 'But don't tell all the others—I can't feed the whole zoo!'

Anna didn't mind the insult as long as she had

the sweet. They watched her as she tested it with her teeth.

'Yum!' she said. 'I've tasted worse. Where did you get them, Mike?'

The rest of the day was notable for the number of times when more sweets could be eaten, and when the bell rang at the end of the afternoon Jason owed Michael four sweets and so did Selwyn, and Anna had promised to repay him with three. All of them made a beeline for the sweetshop in Chase Road after school. They stood with their noses pressed against the window, but they couldn't see any of the new sweets on display. All the boxes and jars contained the usual well-known brands, and Taste Bud Ticklers and Mind Bogglers were not to be seen.

'Are you sure you bought them here?' asked Anna. 'You're not kidding, are you?'

'Of course not,' said Mike, puzzled. 'If I had any more money, I'd go in and buy some.'

'I've only 10p—' began Jason.

'I have 10p too,' put in Anna. 'What about you, Selwyn? If we put our money together, I can go in and ask for a bagful, and we can share them.'

Selwyn searched in his pockets, and triumphantly came out with 10p.

'Which sort do you like best?' asked Anna.

'It doesn't matter,' said Jason, handing over his coin.

'Buy anything you like.' Selwyn agreed.

Anna disappeared into the shop, and the boys waited. Mike frowned. Suppose Anna came out and said that none of the new sweets was there? He felt the remaining ones in his pockets to help him believe he really had bought them and that he wasn't dreaming.

Anna came rushing out of the shop.

'They're all there!' she cried. 'I've bought some different ones—Lip Smackers, these are called. Try one, all of you.'

They did so, and there was a busy silence for a few seconds as they chewed and passed judgement on the Lip Smackers.

'Great,' said Michael. 'You can repay me with some of those, if you like.'

'You'll have to wait until tomorrow,' replied Jason. 'I'll try and get an advance on my pocket money and give you back the same ones as you gave me.'

The next day each of them had found some more money. Anna had borrowed some from her brother, Jason had sold a model car to a friend, and Selwyn begged an extra thirty pence from his mother. Michael was paid back for his loans in the playground—but in the meantime the news about the new sweetshop had spread. Four children with pockets full of sweets can't easily hide them from their classmates for long—and several other members of the class had discovered the shop and the new brands of sweets for themselves.

Mr Browser had never been faced with such an outbreak of chewing in class before, nor had Class 8 been so inattentive.

'If I see anyone else eating sweets in class, or even looking at them, I shall have to take the whole bag away for the rest of the day,' he warned them.

In spite of the warning, Jason couldn't resist rustling his bag of sweets in his pocket, trying to work out how many he had left.

'Bring them out, Jason!' demanded Mr Browser. 'I'll look after them for you.'

When the time for the short afternoon break came, Jason pleaded for his sweets.

'I won't eat another one of them in class, Mr Browser, I promise,' he said, and Mr Browser weakened and let him have them back.

The afternoon was fine, and Mr Sage, the Headmaster, being in a jolly mood still because he had holed out in one at golf during the holiday, toured the playground and meddled with groups playing football and hopscotch. Catching sight of Jason's bag of sweets, he darted across and picked one from the bag.

'May I?' he asked politely before unwrapping the sweet.

Most children, especially the younger ones, took it to be an honour if Mr Sage fancied one of their sweets, and he was a little surprised to find that Jason didn't look exactly delighted.

'Must be something special,' he joked, and read the wrapping paper. 'Lip Smackers! Never heard of them,' he said, and unwrapped the sweet and popped it in his mouth. 'Yum, yum,' he added. 'Interesting taste! I can see why you didn't want to part with it, Jason. Many thanks!' Off he went on his tour of the playground, then went back into school, where he met Mr Browser.

'Unusual sweets your class have, George. Never tasted anything like them before.'

'They're a proper nuisance,' declared Mr Browser. 'The children can't leave them alone. It seems they come from the shop in Chase Road which has just re-opened.'

'You ought to try them,' said Mr Sage, and went to his room to sit down for a while, because he had suddenly become giddy for just a moment or two.

Mr Browser was only too pleased when the bell for the end of afternoon school rang. It seemed to him that he had been spending all his time trying to persuade his class to listen and to get on with their work—though the lesson he had been giving had been a success for many long years. There was only one obvious reason for Class 8's poor attention—

their minds were concentrating on the sweets which even Mr Sage had praised. Maybe it was only the novelty of the sweets which was the cause of the unrest, thought Mr Browser hopefully—but he was doubtful enough about this to decide that it would be interesting to stop at the shop on his way home and buy his wife a box of chocolates.

He drove home by way of Chase Road and pulled up outside the shop. Like the children before him, he could see nothing unusual about the window display. He decided on the popular brand of chocolates he would buy, and entered the shop. Behind the counter was an elderly lady he recognised at once; she had served in a number of shops in Chivvy Chase over the years.

'Good afternoon, Mrs Beacon. So you've opened up here again. Some of your sweets are very popular with my children at school.'

'These, I expect, Mr Browser,' she replied, pointing to the trays of Lip Smackers, Taste Bud Ticklers, Mind Bogglers and Telly Mates which were placed in front of the counter. 'They're new—obtained by the new owner, Mr Smith. I've tried some of them myself—I like the Telly Mates best, they seem to make the T.V. programmes more interesting. Why not try some, Mr Browser?'

'I think I'll settle for a box of chocolates,' said Mr Browser, indicating which one he wanted.

As she fetched the box, the door at the back of the shop opened and a pale, youngish man, his face half hidden behind huge tortoiseshell glasses, appeared.

'Mr Smith—this is Mr Browser, a teacher at Chivvy Chase School,' said Mrs Beacon. 'Mr Browser, this is the new owner, Mr Smith.'

'Pleased to meet you, Mr Smith,' said Mr Browser. 'I was telling Mrs Beacon what a hit your sweets have made with my children. Made by a new firm, aren't they?'

'Indeed they are,' said Mr Smith. 'They come from a new factory I've discovered. Made in Britain, of course. As a matter of fact, I'm a teacher myself. I'm new to the area, and I'm looking to fill in for teachers who may fall ill—that's until I find a full-time place in a school. Mrs Beacon will be able to run the shop on her own by then. You don't know of any vacancies, do you?'

'Not at the moment,' said Mr Browser. 'If I were you, I'd contact Mr Sage, the Headmaster. He's always interested to hear of supply teachers.'

'Supply teachers, ah, yes,' said Mr Smith, as though he'd forgotten the word. 'Thank you for your help. By the way, why don't you try one of these? The salesman left a few with me this afternoon, and I think they'll be very popular. It's a kind of marzipan.'

He went to a cupboard and produced a large, round, brown sweet sitting on a piece of silver paper.

'What do you think of it?' he asked, as Mr Browser put it in his mouth and reduced it to a better size for eating.

'Most unusual,' he said, when he could speak. 'Tastes of a mixture of strawberries and raspberries—and there's a touch of peaches, as well. Most extraordinary.'

'Glad you like it,' said Mr Smith, and left them as silently as he had appeared.

Mr Browser drove home and was well received with his box of chocolates. He was so impressed with the new sweet that he regretted not asking what it was called, and thought about going to the shop and buying some more the next day. But when it came to it, he shied away from entering the sweet-shop before school. As he drove past it, he saw a number of Chivvy Chase children, including some from his own class, entering the shop or coming out with sweets. He arrived at school fearful of another disturbed day, and he was right to be afraid.

Class 8 was more talkative than usual, more fidgety than usual, and even less attentive than the day before.

'Don't let me set eyes on any of those sweets!' threatened Mr Browser, and his threat only

irritated his pupils more. By playtime he was feeling, as he put it to Mr Sage, 'definitely under the weather'.

The Headmaster was as sympathetic as a Headmaster can be who is faced with having to fill a gap in the classroom if a teacher falls ill.

'If you feel any worse, you'd better go straight home,' he said. 'What exactly is the matter?'

'I feel odd—it could be 'flu,' Mr Browser tried to explain—he wasn't used to being unwell, except sometimes at weekends. 'Slight headache, and at times the children's faces seem to swim in front of my eyes. Mind, the children have been rather difficult for the past two days. Can't concentrate on anything except sweets.'

'Things do get difficult if you're not on form yourself,' said Mr Sage, and left Mr Browser wondering whether that was sympathy or criticism.

Almost as soon as Mr Sage had sat down in his room, his telephone rang.

'A gentleman on the phone,' said Miss Copewell from the office. 'Says he would like to do some supply teaching, if ever we need someone.'

'Put him through,' Mr Sage told her. 'Spare teachers are like gold dust.'

The gentleman on the phone explained that he had just come into the district, hoped to become a full-time teacher, and would be pleased to help out if ever needed. Mr Sage chatted to him for a while, then took his name and address. He put the phone down and went to see Miss Copewell in the office.

'Make a note of this name and address, please,' he asked her. 'It's good to have someone ready to step in if someone's ill. Old George Browser isn't looking too good. I'll go and see how he's getting on.'

Poor old George Browser was wiping perspiration from his forehead with a handkerchief and telling Michael Fairlie off for eating sweets in class at the same time. Now Mr Sage felt really sorry for him.

'By the way,' he said, 'I've just had an offer of supply teaching from Mr Smith of Chase Road. Sounds a reasonable fellow. If things get worse, let me know and I'll fetch him in for this afternoon. No point in trying to teach if you're not up to it.'

'I'd be grateful,' said Mr Browser. 'I'm all hot and sticky. Never felt like this before. Smith, did you say? He lives above the sweetshop in Chase Road. I had a chat with him yesterday. Very pale looking man—wears huge horn-rimmed glasses.'

Mr Sage was not at all concerned about the appearance of a possible new teacher, as long as he didn't have spiky, dyed hair and big earrings.

'Try and carry on until lunch time,' he told Mr Browser, 'and I'll ring him back now. We're lucky to have him, because Mrs Cunnington, our usual supply, is away on holiday. I'll let you know if he can come.'

By twelve o'clock Mr Browser was so unwell that even if Mr Smith hadn't been able to come and take the class, he could not have gone on teaching. Mr Sage was now most helpful.

'Don't hurry back, George,' he said. 'Make sure you're properly fit before you return. If I were you, I'd go home to bed at once.'

Mr Browser agreed, and drove home feeling unwell, but also suspicious that something strange was going on, something connected with the sweet-shop in Chase Road. However, when he arrived home his wife quickly convinced him that he was most unwell, so he went to bed and forgot all about the sweetshop and Mr Smith.

And so Mr Sage was able to introduce Class 8 to their new teacher, Mr Smith, that afternoon. Mr Sage brought him into the classroom.

'Unfortunately Mr Browser has been taken ill,' said Mr Sage, 'but very fortunately Mr Smith has come to take his place. You'll find them a set of hardworking children, Mr Smith. If there's anything you want, please let me know. I shall expect all you children to be helpful to Mr Smith. I shall be keeping an eye on you myself from time to time.'

With a final glare warning them that they had better be helpful and hardworking, or expect the worst, the Headmaster left them in the care of the new teacher, who opened his briefcase and looked inside it.

'He looks like a figure from the waxworks,' whispered Anna. 'His glasses must be as big as the ones that snooker player wears.'

Mr Smith snapped his briefcase to and stared at the class.

'Now that I am your teacher I shall expect hard work in the important subjects,' he said. His words were clipped and clear, as if a typewriter had spoken them.

'What's wrong with Mr Browser, please?' called out Michael. 'You won't be our teacher for long, will you?'

'Who knows how long Mr Browser will be away,' said Mr Smith, frowning. 'That's something we don't need to be thinking about at the moment. Before we start work, I must tell you that I happen to know that a number of you have bought sweets from a shop in Chase Road. Now I don't want you to be trying to eat sweets in class time, tasty though they may be—so I'm going to give out one sweet to each of you straight away. Eat that, and then forget about sweets until playtime and after school.'

As they watched in amazed silence, Mr Smith

walked stiffly round the classroom giving each child a Mind Boggler.

'Maybe he isn't so bad after all,' muttered Jason Little to Michael. 'Old Browser would never do anything like that.'

'It's a bit odd,' commented Selwyn Jordan, who always thought twice before acting—but the Mind Boggler was too tempting, and he unwrapped it and put it in his mouth.

'Now,' said Mr Smith, when he had toured the whole class, 'we can start the first lesson.'

'The first lesson is P.E.,' called out Jason.

Mr Smith's head jerked back a little, and he frowned again.

'Please don't call out,' he told Jason. 'The first lesson with me is not P.E.—it's learning your tables. I believe in standards, and we are going to achieve them. Write me out the six times table in your maths books.'

'But—' began Anna.

'I know it already,' declared Selwyn.

'Silence!' thundered the new teacher. 'You've had your sweets, now do as I say!'

All that afternoon Class 8 slogged away at tables and spellings, sometimes going over and over facts and figures they knew already. At three o'clock Michael Fairlie made his protest.

'Please Mr Smith, we're watching a series of T.V.

programmes about birds and their eggs, and it's due to start now!'

'We have no time for such programmes,' insisted Mr Smith. 'All I require is that you should be able to add up, take away, know your tables and spell a certain number of words. Little more is expected of you. I don't want to hear any more suggestions for lessons. At the end of the day I'll give you each another sweet, but only if you work well.'

By the end of the afternoon they were all bored and weary. They wanted to relax and they hated having to concentrate, but Mr Smith held them in a stern mental grip. Their minds and spirits were dulled as he brought around the farewell sweets. When he came to Michael Fairlie, he noticed that there was an empty seat next to Michael.

'Who sits there?' he asked.

'That's Spiky—I mean, Simon Jackson's place,' said Michael. 'He's away on holiday in Spain. He won't be back until next week.'

'Is that so!' said Mr Smith, and looked far from pleased. The bell rang, and he dismissed the class. They all ran wildly out of the school, disturbing Mr Sage in his room and frightening some of the smaller children as they walked down the path to the gate. Jason Little and some others made straight for the sweetshop to buy some more sweets, while Michael and Anna and Selwyn hurried home to watch T.V. Mr Sage went to Mr Browser's room to see how the new teacher had been doing.

'A good beginning, I think, Mr Sage,' said Mr Smith. 'After a few days I think I shall have them where I want them.'

Mr Sage didn't ask where that might be—he was pleased to find Mr Smith in determined mood. He knew that Class 8 was not an easy class for a new teacher to deal with, and he was happy to see that Mr Smith had kept them under control.

'Good work,' he said, 'keep it up.'

'I certainly will,' declared Mr Smith, and closed his briefcase and went home to his flat over the shop. He greeted Mrs Beacon briefly, went upstairs and quietly locked himself in the flat. He made at once for his bedroom and carefully took down a large case from the top of his wardrobe. He put the case on the bed and opened it. The case was almost filled by a large black box, which he lifted carefully out and placed on a small table by the window. He brought up a chair and opened the box by pressing a button which lifted the lid. On the underside of the lid was some writing which looked like a mixture of Ancient Egyptian hieroglyphics, Japanese and Arabic. He took a close look at this for at least a minute, then stood up and opened the window as wide as it would go. Then he sat down and began pressing various parts of the box, which was solid and divided into dozens of little squares, each with a sign on it.

An expression of pleasure appeared on the waxy face of Mr Smith. Class 8's new teacher was behaving exactly as if he were a spy sending secret messages to an unknown power.

3
The Mind Shrinkers' Master Plan

It is not often that a sun is encircled by two planets on which forms of life can exist. This did happen in the case of the planet of the Mind Shrinkers and that of the Brain Sharpeners. The Brain Sharpeners developed earlier than the Mind Shrinkers, and as they were by nature peaceful creatures, they spent little time in exploration until an increase in their population and a big advance in their knowledge of science convinced them that they ought to try and discover other planets to develop.

The Brain Sharpeners have large heads—and brains—and so need plenty of the right atmosphere in which to live. They discovered that the Mind Shrinkers were having a hard time of it on a planet very short of oxygen, and therefore they ignored them. As some may know, they found that the atmosphere on Earth had proved suitable for life, and they tried to sharpen the brains of the humans so that they could be used as slaves when suitable planets were found. Unfortunately after several attempts they decided that young humans, particularly Class 8 of Chivvy Chase School, were not easy subjects for brain sharpening, and after a while they dropped their plans for them.

Meanwhile the Mind Shrinkers, made tough in mind and body by trying to exist on their stony planet, on which the air was so thin that life could barely survive, had reached the stage when they could travel out into space and also spy on their neighbours, the Brain Sharpeners. The history of the Mind Shrinkers was not an exciting one. They began as blobs of jelly-like cells which fitted into holes and cracks on the surface of their planet, where they found protection against the scorching heat of their summer sun, and against the icy winter winds. Gradually, as they became stronger, they grew short arms and legs, and scuttled from place to place in search of food. When at last their brains were big enough for them to realise that they were living on a small, none too pleasant planet, they gave all their energy to space exploration, and for a while had plans to invade the planet of the Brain Sharpeners. When they realised the Brain Sharpeners were too sharp for them, they decided to make use of the Brain Sharpeners, and spied on their attempts to sharpen up human brains at Chivvy Chase School. They realised that the Brain Sharpeners, hard though they had tried, had failed in this, and so they decided to make an all-out attempt to do the opposite—to shrink the minds of

the humans and soften them up so that they would allow themselves to be taken over without protest. If the Brain Sharpeners had failed at Chivvy Chase, then that was the place for the Mind Shrinkers to succeed!

They would reduce them to mental slavery, and they would carry out early tests at Chivvy Chase School. The Mind Shrinkers had been unable to improve themselves for many years because in the old days their ancestors had eaten the fruit of a plant which had weakened their minds; only when the mind shrinking nature of the plant had been discovered, and the population had been forbidden to eat its fruit, had progress been made. Now large stocks of the mind shrinking plant were stored ready for use on human beings when the time came.

By means of brain transplants over the years a small body of clever scientists was created, who secretly borrowed ideas from the Brain Sharpeners and could make space craft which could study behaviour on Earth. Finally, by grafting cells together a Mind Shrinker was created who could pass as a human being, if a rather pale and waxy one. This was Mr Smith, who was landed one night and made his way to Chivvy Chase, where he lived as a student in lodgings, paid for by the DHSS, for a while. All the time he was supposed to be studying for the Open University, he was really studying people, and particularly the children of Chivvy Chase School. From time to time he sent messages back, reporting on what he thought would be the best way of encouraging children to eat the mind shrinking fruit.

Sweets were the obvious answer, and so large numbers of Mind Bogglers, Taste Bud Ticklers, Lip Smackers and Telly Mates were manufactured by the Mind Shrinkers, under instruction from Mr Smith, who told them how earthly sweets were wrapped and the size which was most likely to suit the human mouth. Then, with the forged money he had brought with him, Mr Smith bought the Chase Road sweetshop—and his campaign had begun. The children came into the shop and soon the news of the strange tasting sweets spread around. Mr Smith reported that all was going well, but that in order to check on the progress being made he was hoping to make closer contact with the children by becoming their teacher for a time. When Mr Browser played into his hands by trying a sweet especially made to bring on a high fever, he sent an enthusiastic message back to report that all was going very well.

The Mind Shrinkers were pleased to learn that their spy was being successful, but he did not know that he formed only a part of their plans. They held meetings at which their scientists put forward various other ways of deadening human minds, and they agreed upon several. One was by sending rays through T.V. aerials to cause a kind of hypnotism to set in when people watched certain programmes. Serial programmes, they decided, were ideal for this purpose, especially as they would reach a very large number of people. This method was to be developed for use just before the invasion. Another and slower way, which would start earlier, would be to spray the fields with a liquid form of mind-shrinking material, similar to that used in the sweets, which would then be absorbed by people when they ate crops or fruit and drank milk.

The actual invasion of the Mind Shrinkers would only take place when human minds had been lowered to a standard at which people no longer wanted to think for themselves, but would accept the kind of life offered to them by the Mind Shrinkers. When the Mind Shrinkers dropped from the sky, in shapes designed for speedy movement, they would quickly take charge of all the important centres, disguising themselves as humans where necessary. In less than a year human beings would become the slaves of the Mind Shrinkers, forced to eat what the Mind Shrinkers provided and offered only the kind of programmes on T.V. which could be watched without thinking.

But before any of this could happen, they had to be sure that the experiment at Chivvy Chase School was a success. Some argued that they could accept the word of Mr Smith, but many were against trusting in one Mind Shrinker, and demanded that the children of Class 8 be brought in front of them so that all could see their mental state.

A vote was taken, and Mr Smith was told that the children in his class, when their minds were sufficiently shrunken, were to be picked up by space craft and brought to the home base. Mr Smith protested that this would be difficult to organise, and pleaded that the tests be carried out on Earth.

'Besides, they're not ready yet,' he insisted. 'Too many of them are still thinking for themselves.'

'There's no hurry,' came the reply. 'Take your time and do a thorough job. We must make certain that we can settle on Earth. There we shall be far enough away from the Brain Sharpeners to be able to live happily and defend ourselves successfully. Perform your task well and you will be awarded a Mind Shrinker First Class Medal. Fail, and there will be no need for you to return.'

The Mind Shrinkers had only survived through being ruthless, and Mr Smith knew that they meant what they said. Therefore he became ruthless with

Class 8, narrowing their minds down as much as possible and now and then feeding them with Mind Bogglers and Taste Bud Ticklers over and above those they bought for themselves.

Mr Sage was very pleased with his supply teacher. The class appeared to be working well, and Mr Smith was in complete control of them.

'What a lucky break that I found him,' he said to Miss Copewell. 'Poor old George Browser doesn't seem to be any better, but we can afford to let him take his time to recover.'

'Mr Smith is a funny man,' said Miss Copewell. 'He doesn't go into the staffroom much, and he never drinks tea. I've never seen him eat or drink anything, come to think of it.'

'That's really nothing to do with us,' declared the Headmaster. 'As long as he keeps them working, I'm happy.'

Of course, not only the children of Chivvy Chase School came into the sweetshop and bought the mind-shrinking sweets supplied by Mr Smith. Young mothers with toddlers and children of nursery school age were not slow to discover that a course of Mind Bogglers made their lives much easier. After eating a few of the sweets the noisiest toddlers cut down on their tantrums, and the biggest nuisances became well behaved and even helpful. Mr Smith was so pleased that he signalled to his leaders that if he had the money he would be able to open another shop, and maybe in time a chain of shops all over the country. Secretly he hoped that his masters would then appoint him as Chief Mind Shrinker for the whole area; and he was rather disappointed when they said nothing in reply to his signals, except to remind him to concentrate on the children of Class 8 so that they could be examined before the return of Mr Browser.

Progress with Class 8 was steady, but not without its awkward moments. It would take plenty of Mind Bogglers and Telly Mates to turn such as Anna Cardwell into quiet, obedient puppets. In spite of all the sweets she had eaten, now and again she burst out in protest.

'Please, Mr Smith, must we do maths and English all the time? We used to watch the nature programme with Mr Browser. Are we going to do that this week?'

'There will be no time for such lessons,' Mr Smith told her, 'until your spellings are a hundred per cent correct and your work in the main subjects pleases me. Please do not put such questions to me again!'

Sometimes Anna's outbursts roused a little life in some of the others.

'But Mr Smith!' called out Michael. 'We haven't

had one P.E. lesson this week—'

'Enough!' barked Mr Smith. 'I have to bring you up to a certain standard, and that I will do. What you did with Mr Browser is no concern of mine, nor of yours, indeed. Down to work, and no more calling out!'

Gradually as the days passed, Class 8 came to accept Mr Smith's way of teaching without question, and even seemed happy to do without games, P.E., art and T.V. lessons. Mr Smith began to relax, and the oily smile appeared on his face more often, and his eyes gleamed from behind his glasses. The other teachers found him somewhat odd, but they were pleased not to have to teach Mr Browser's class as well as their own. What's more, they found their own classes easier to teach in some ways, because, of course, plenty of sweets from the Chase Road shop were being eaten by all classes at Chivvy Chase School.

A curious and unfortunate idea formed in the Headmaster's mind. Since Mr Browser's illness, he decided, the school had been a quieter place altogether. Could it be that this was the result of Mr Browser's absence? He decided to ring up Mrs Browser.

'Hello, Mrs Browser. Mr Sage here. Could you tell me how George is getting on?'

'He's much better, thank you,' she replied. 'But he's never had an attack quite like this before, and he's still feeling very weak, and I don't think he'll be able to return to school for some days yet.'

'I'm sorry,' said Mr Sage, 'but I'm glad to hear he's feeling better. Tell him there's no need for him to hurry back.'

When he put down the receiver he didn't look sorry at all, in fact he rubbed his hands together with some satisfaction. Then he took a stroll in the direction of Class 8, and as he neared the classroom he heard the comforting sound of tables being chanted. After listening to this for a while, he decided to go and tell Mr Smith that he would certainly be required for a few more days, maybe longer.

'Mrs Browser is not sure when her husband will be fit to return,' he informed him. 'Meanwhile, keep up the good work. Class 8 seem to have taken to you, and I have to admit that these children have been known to make life difficult for one or two young teachers.'

'Thank you, Mr Sage,' said Mr Smith, passing a smooth white hand over his sleek black hair. 'It's just that I demand high standards, that's all.'

And feed them on Mind Bogglers, he secretly thought.

'Good,' said Mr Sage. 'By the way, where is Simon Jackson?'

'His parents have taken him on holiday to Spain, Mr Sage,' called out Anna. 'He'll be back on Monday.'

'You'll find him a lively lad,' declared the Headmaster to Mr Smith. 'It's a pity he's missed this week.'

'Oh, I'm sure he'll soon fit in,' said Mr Smith, with all the confidence of someone who had never met Spiky Jackson.

4

The Return of Spiky Jackson

Spiky Jackson's holiday on the Costa del Sol in Spain was not a complete success. The flight to Malaga was no novelty, as Spiky had been flying to hot countries for holidays since he was one year old. His mum and dad were keen sunbathers, happy to stretch out in the sun for most of every day, so Spiky was often left to his own devices.

Inviting though the sea was on most days, you can grow tired of swimming, and the beach was too crowded for the kind of running, jumping and chasing games which Spiky favoured. His companions, too, were not ideal. One was a boy a year older than Spiky, who was very determined to organise everything his way, and had a little sister who kept on getting in the way, yelling when she was knocked over. Spiky found himself wishing for the company of his friends at Chivvy Chase, where at least he was respected.

The sun was too hot at times, and the food didn't always agree with him. Also the T.V. programmes were in Spanish, which was most annoying. So by the end of the fortnight he was beginning to look forward to the return home, and was happy to board the coach which took them to the airport at Malaga. The plane was due to leave at seven o'clock at night, but for some reason there was a delay, and so Spiky spent the next two and a half hours in the Departure Lounge trying to behave himself but not always succeeding. Finally the plane took off at ten o'clock Spanish time, and the Jackson family only arrived home at one o'clock on Monday morning.

Spiky was therefore none too pleased to be awakened by his mum seven hours later and told to hurry up or he'd be late for school. In spite of her best efforts, she couldn't make Spiky move very fast, and he left the house at quarter to nine. The walk to school usually took him a quarter of an hour, so he knew he would have to run part of the way in order to avoid being late on his first day back at school. He arrived in the playground at one minute to nine, and by the time he had found Michael Fairlie the school bell rang, a whistle was blown and all talking had to stop.

So Spiky went into school knowing nothing about Mr Browser's illness or about the new teacher, Mr Smith, nor was he aware of the Mind Bogglers, Taste Bud Ticklers, Telly Mates and Lip Smackers.

'Who's this?' he asked Michael when the new teacher strode into the room.

'It's Mr Smith,' explained Michael in a whisper.

'Browser's ill, and this one's taken over. He makes us work hard, but he gives us sweets.'

'Gives you sweets?' asked Spiky, and as he looked around the class a strange unease overcame him. All his friends—and friendly enemies—were so quiet and well behaved. Panic made his heart beat a little faster. Was school really like this? Had the holiday in Spain made him forget what life was really like? Surely the rest of the day wouldn't pass in a hush like this?

'Mike!' he whispered. 'Is this teacher really so strict—'

'Stand up, the boy who spoke!' demanded Mr Smith sharply, and as all heads were turned towards him, Spiky obeyed. 'Oh yes, it's Simon Jackson,' went on the new teacher, smiling his oiliest smile. 'I trust you had an enjoyable holiday, Simon. I am Mr Smith, and you'll find there have been some changes since you went on holiday. We are concentrating on important matters, and there isn't any time for talking in class—except when I say so. However, don't worry, you'll soon fit in, I'm sure. Now—join the others in writing down the thirty words for spelling which I have written on the blackboard, while I call the register.'

There was silence in Class 8 until the bell rang for Assembly. It was something of a relief to Spiky to see that Mr Sage was still there, leading the

Assembly in the usual way and ending up with his frequent warning about the leaving of litter in the playground. But all too soon he was back in the classroom, waiting with the rest of the class for the next move by Mr. Smith.

The teacher took a tin out of his briefcase, and Spiky noticed that his classmates were sitting up straight, as eager as dogs on their hind legs begging for a titbit of food. Mr Smith opened the tin and poured out a pile of sweets.

'Come out, the usual helpers,' he ordered, and Jason Little, Anna Cardwell, Barry Sibbet and Angela Gilpin moved swiftly to his desk. 'Today it's Taste Bud Ticklers,' he said, and a kind of sigh of anticipation came from the class.

'Why does he give you these sweets, Mike?' asked Spiky—but Mr Smith rapped on his desk with a ruler before Michael could reply.

'No talking in class!' he thundered. 'Simon Jackson, I have warned you once, and if you don't take notice, I shall have to take action. Don't interrupt the lesson again!'

'Lesson!' muttered Spiky, but very quietly because Mr Smith was glaring at him so intensely.

The helpers meanwhile were picking up the sweets and counting them, and then they walked around the classroom handing one to each child. Mr Smith sat watchfully at his desk as the sweet papers were opened and the Taste Bud Ticklers popped swiftly into eager mouths. Spiky was about to do the same when Anna handed him one, but something in the teacher's look made him hesitate. Why, he wondered, is Mr Smith so keen that all the sweets should be eaten? Maybe, he thought, they contained some kind of drug. He decided against eating his, but saw the teacher's eyes upon him.

Swiftly he carried out the kind of trick with his hands which is often used to deceive young children. He pretended to take the sweet from his left hand into his right, and then brought his hand up to his mouth. Mr Smith appeared satisfied, and Spiky added to the effect by chewing at an imaginary sweet for the next few minutes.

After that the day went on its dreary way—a succession of sums and spellings, grammar and handwriting, with no relief at all. What disturbed Spiky most was that the rest of the class appeared pleased to accept all this, and didn't even make any requests for games or P.E. or a T.V. programme. Spiky fell in with them, but burst out into the playground at lunch time with a frenzy of energy.

'How can you sit there like a set of waxwork models all day long?' he demanded of Anna Cardwell, who had formerly always been a restless pupil. 'You're not natural any more!'

'Don't be silly, Spiky,' replied Anna, 'we like it the

way it is. Old Browser never used to give us any sweets!'

'Sweets!' burst out Spiky. 'Can't you see—it's the sweets that are doing it!'

'Doing what?' asked Anna, looking innocent.

'I give up!' declared Spiky, and went and bounced a tennis ball against the wall until it was time to eat.

'Have a Mind Boggler,' said Michael Fairlie, joining him and offering him an open bag of sweets. 'Come on, they taste great!' he added as Spiky hesitated. The temptation was great.

'Where did you buy them?' he asked, as a delaying tactic.

'Of course, you don't know about the sweetshop in Chase Road,' said Michael. 'We all buy our sweets there since it opened last week. That's where Mr Smith gets his—he lives in the flat over the shop. They're super sweets, Spiky. You've been missing something.'

'Looks as though I have,' agreed Spiky, 'but I won't have one now, thanks. I don't want to spoil my dinner.'

'All the more for me,' said Michael, surprised by this most un-Spikylike behaviour. He put the bag of sweets in his pocket and ran off.

After that Spiky was determined not to eat any of the sweets until he had made his own investigations. The afternoon passed as drearily for him as the morning had done. The tireless Mr Smith gave out information from books and from the blackboard, and Class 8 took it all in without a murmur. Each time Spiky tried to speak he was jumped on by Mr Smith, and he very soon decided to keep quiet and fall in with the rest, so as not to arouse the teacher's anger and suspicions.

At the end of the afternoon, as they took the path to the school gate, he made a final appeal to his old friends.

'Mike, you don't really like being taught by this Smith man, do you? I know you're learning plenty, but it's dull stuff. You might as well grow up to be a calculator. You won't know much about the world. At least learning was sometimes fun with old Browser. Are you going to carry on like this? I don't think I shall be able to stand it.'

'You missed the first week, Spiky,' replied Michael. 'You'll soon get used to Smithy and his ways.'

Smithy! Now Michael was talking as if he really liked the creature. Spiky gave a snort of disgust and ran off. He felt lonely and deserted, as if all his old friends had suddenly gone out of his life. Surely the holiday in Spain couldn't be to blame for all this? Spiky wondered if he should ask his mum to have him transferred to another school. There was a lot of talk lately, he knew, about parents having the power to choose the school which their children should attend. He was gloomily thinking that his mum probably would take a great deal of persuading, because apart from Chivvy Chase there was no other school within easy reach of his home, and she wouldn't want to have to drive him to school—when there in front of him was Mr Browser, strolling slowly towards him and looking rather pale. Spiky's spirits rose. Why be so downhearted when probably old Browser would be back at school again soon!

'Hello, Mr Browser!' he called out. 'Are you feeling better? Will you be coming back to school soon?'

Mr Browser was pleased, if a little surprised, to hear that Spiky was interested in his return. This, he thought, must mean that the new supply teacher was either very strict or was not allowing Spiky enough time for sport.

'I'm feeling much better, Sp—er, Simon,' he replied. 'I must say, I've never had such a bad attack of 'flu before, but at last I can walk about a little now. I hope I'll be back at school in two or three days. Thank you for asking. Did you have a good time on holiday?'

'Yes, thank you, Mr Browser. But it's awful in

school at the moment—no games, no art, no P.E., no T.V., only maths and English, and some science from books. It's boring, Mr Browser!'

Mr Browser looked at Spiky with some sympathy, for he'd never seen the boy so dispirited before. However, it was not for him to comment on a fellow teacher.

'Never mind, Simon. No doubt it's all to the good. If you've learned such a lot while I've been away, maybe I can fit in an extra games lesson when I come back.'

He started to walk away, and Spiky called after him. 'Do come back soon, Mr Browser, please!'

'Well, well,' thought Mr Browser, 'what's come over the boy? I've never known him like this before. Whatever can Smith be doing with them? If only I felt a little stronger, I'd go back to school tomorrow!'

When Spiky entered the classroom the next day he had a faint hope that Mr Browser might have changed his mind and come back to school after all. Then in walked Mr Smith, blinking at them through his thick-rimmed glasses and smiling his usual crocodile smile. He dumped his case on the desk, and soon the ration of sweets was being given out by his willing helpers.

'It's Mind Bogglers today!' whispered Anna. 'I think I like them best of all.'

As she popped the Mind Boggler into her mouth, Spiky put his in his pocket.

'Make the most of them while you can,' he told Anna. 'I met Browser yesterday, and he's getting better. He'll be back soon, and then you'll have to buy your own Mind Bogglers, if you must have them.'

'Stand up, that boy who spoke!' demanded Mr Smith who seemed to have highly tuned ears. Spiky delayed for a moment, but again his former friends turned to look at him, so he gave in and stood up, pretending to chew his Mind Boggler as he did so.

'Ah! Simon Jackson, the boy who's been away on holiday. Kindly repeat exactly what you said to Anna Cardwell, please.'

'It was nothing,' replied Spiky, trying to gain time.

'Exactly what you said, please,' repeated Mr Smith coldly, and his eyes looked at Spiky like those of a hungry shark.

'I only told Anna to make the most of her Mind Bogglers,' he said.

'You said more than that,' declared Mr Smith. 'And why should she make the most of her Mind Bogglers?'

Something made a warning signal flash in Spiky's head, and he felt it could be dangerous to tell Mr Smith about Mr Browser's planned return.

'I don't know,' he answered sullenly.

'Don't know?' This time Mr Smith showed nearly all of his even white teeth as he smiled. 'I shall deal with you later, boy. Now, Anna Cardwell, tell me exactly what he said to you.'

'Please, Mr Smith, he said I'd better make the most of the sweets because Mr Browser would be coming back soon, and then I'd have to buy my own.'

Mr Smith's face looked as white as a candle in daylight, and he turned away from the class for a few seconds. When he faced them again, he spoke to Spiky.

'And what makes you think he might return?'

Spiky realised there could be no point in remaining silent any longer.

'I met Mr Browser yesterday afternoon. He was out for a walk, and he said he was feeling better. I said I hoped he'd be back soon, Mr Smith.'

Spiky sat down as if that were the end of the matter. Mr Smith appeared about to speak angrily, but changed his mind.

'Continue with your work,' he said. 'There is no time to waste.'

The class settled happily to work, and Spiky pretended to follow the example of the others. From time to time Mr Smith stared hard at Spiky, as though he wished he would disappear. The

morning passed uneasily for Spiky, but in spite of all his threatening looks the teacher took no action. At twelve o'clock he hurried out of the room as soon as the class was dismissed. He paced down the corridor and knocked impatiently on the Headmaster's door.

'Come in,' Mr Sage called. 'Ah, Mr Smith—all going well, I trust?'

'Very well,' replied Mr Smith. 'The boy who has just come back from holiday seems slow to settle down, but apart from that I've no complaints.'

'Yes, I'm not surprised,' said Mr Sage. 'Simon Jackson is not the world's keenest learner. However, keep a strict eye on him and he'll be all right.'

'I'm sure he will,' agreed Mr Smith. 'I came to ask you, Mr Sage, if you've heard any news of Mr Browser. I hear he's been seen out walking.'

'Has he? Well, he has to convalesce, I suppose. No, I haven't rung him for several days. I don't like to disturb him, and there's no urgency while we have you with us, is there?'

The Headmaster smiled and almost winked, but controlled his eyelid just in time.

'Nice of you to say so, Mr Sage,' said Mr Smith, and went away a little relieved. Nevertheless, he went home to the sweetshop very quickly that afternoon and set his message machine into position.

His report to the Mind Shrinkers informed his masters that all was going well. He hinted that one or two children still had to be worked upon, but he didn't mention Spiky by name. He added that the Headmaster must have eaten a Mind Boggler or two, probably taken from the children at playtimes, and thanks to that was in no mood to hurry the return of Mr Browser. The Chief Mind Shrinker praised Mr Smith for his report, but added the warning that the inspection of the children would have to take place soon. 'The eating of sweets may be effective with children, but clearly we shall have to attack the grown-ups with a different weapon—probably by means of their T.V. screens. Once we have conquered the people by shock methods, and completed our invasion, we shall be able to keep them down by the use of Mind Shrinking foods, and of course sweets for the children. Please report as soon as possible that your children are ready, and a Transparent Transporter will be sent to test them. Tell us exactly where you want it to land, and make it somewhere lonely, where no suspicions are aroused. Remember, you are important to our plans, but not essential! Keep in touch.'

The machine went dead, and Mr Smith found out what a shiver of fear was like. For a moment he almost wished he were not a Mind Shrinker. What a reward, after all his work! His thoughts turned to Spiky Jackson. That boy could stand in the way of his becoming one of the leading Mind Shrinkers of the invasion! He spent some time wondering how best to deal with him, and then went out for a walk, his pockets bulging with Mind Bogglers. Maybe he would meet Spiky and make a present of a bag of them to him. Perhaps he might meet Mr Browser, and persuade him to have another of those sweets which brought on an attack of 'flu. He walked the streets for an hour, but met neither of them. He came home tired and grumbling to himself.

'I'll have to be cleverer,' he kept on telling himself. 'I must keep Browser out of the way, and I must control this boy Simon. Up to now he doesn't seem affected by Mind Bogglers at all.'

Then a thought struck Mr Smith, making him stop dead outside the sweetshop. 'Could it be,' he asked himself, 'that the wretched boy isn't eating the Mind Bogglers I've given him?'

As the likely truth dawned on him, he realised that he could no longer treat Spiky as an awkward pupil—he must be seen as a dangerous enemy! Mr Smith shut himself in his flat and spent the rest of the evening trying to work out plans.

5
The Mr Browser Mystery

The next day, at the giving out of sweets, Mr Smith came and stood over Spiky until the Mind Boggler was unwrapped and safely put into Spiky's mouth. What Mr Smith did not see was that as soon he turned away satisfied, Spiky took it out again and put it in his pocket. That day, and on the following ones, Spiky did his best to please the teacher by his perfect behaviour. The task of keeping quiet and asking no questions was for him an almost superhuman one, but he realised that this was the only way to lull Mr Smith into the belief that he was eating the sweets and becoming just like the rest of the class.

As the days passed and there was no sign of the return of Mr Browser, he feared that his struggle could be in vain. His friends were falling more and more under the spell of Mr Smith—and children in other classes were also being affected by the eating of Mind Bogglers and the other varieties of his sweets. On Friday morning Spiky decided that action must be taken, though he doubted if anything he could do would succeed in shaking the power of Mr Smith.

At playtime he rather nervously walked past Miss Copewell's office and knocked on the Headmaster's door.

'Come in!' came the voice of Mr Sage, and Spiky entered, closing the door behind him. Mr Sage had expected a teacher, or perhaps Miss Copewell bringing in his mid-morning tea, and he was plainly surprised to see Spiky standing in front of him.

'Who sent you here, Simon?' he asked, because usually Spiky appeared as a result of some kind of trouble, either of his own making or of somebody else's.

'No one, Mr Sage. I came myself.'

Mr Sage was suspicious, but tried not to show that he was. 'And what can I do for you?' he asked, smiling in a way that reminded Spiky just a little of Mr Smith. Spiky turned red in the face and looked at the carpet. 'Come along, boy, I haven't all day,' went on Mr Sage, meaning that he was expecting his tea at any moment. Spiky was beginning to wish he'd never come, the matter was so delicate.

'It's—it's about the new teacher,' he began.

'Mr Smith? Have you done something to annoy him?'

Spiky groaned inwardly. This was just the line he thought the Headmaster might take. How could he hope to convince him that Mr Smith was causing

the trouble and not he himself?

'No, Mr Sage. But I don't like what's happening to the class.'

Mr Sage's eyes seemed to pop forward, and he dropped the pencil he was holding.

'Explain yourself, boy!' he demanded. How could Spiky dare to suggest that Class 8 was being taught in the wrong way, when the class was learning hard all day long!

'He gives out sweets,' said Spiky weakly.

'Does he, indeed?' said Mr Sage. 'Well, I'm surprised to hear that you object to that, Simon Jackson!'

'I don't eat them, sir,' said Spiky, and the Headmaster looked puzzled. It's now or never, thought Spiky. 'I think the sweets are poisoning them,' he burst out. 'They're making little robots of them, so that they can't think for themselves any more.'

If a school inspector had said something like this to him, Mr Sage would have listened politely and perhaps have tried to defend the teacher. Coming from Spiky—well, he couldn't believe his ears!

'You're talking nonsense, Simon,' he said, standing up and coming towards Spiky round the side of his desk. 'Eating sweets may not be good for your health, if you eat too many, but I've never heard of eating sweets turning children into robots.'

'But these are different sweets!' protested Spiky. 'Mind Bogglers, Taste Bud Ticklers, Lip Smackers and Telly Mates—they come from the shop where Mr Smith is living. I think he owns it, Mr Sage.'

'How many does he give you in a day?' asked Mr Sage, looking down at Spiky impatiently.

'Only two, usually.'

'Two sweets a day, Simon. Nobody is going to be affected by that. Are you sure the sun in Spain hasn't upset you?'

Spiky was taken aback. At first he had himself wondered whether his holiday had made him different from all the rest—and here was the Headmaster suggesting that maybe the Spanish sun had affected his brain. He stood there speechless, and Mr Sage put a kindly hand on his shoulder.

'Now, Simon, I should join your friends in the playground and forget all about it.'

'Yes, sir,' Spiky obediently turned and made his way into the playground, becoming angrier with himself as he went. He had allowed himself to be put in the wrong, just as he had feared, and Mr Smith was going to be able to carry out his plans unhindered.

'Hello, Spiky,' said Anna when he reached the playground. 'Have a sweet?'

Spiky was tempted. Why not give up and join the rest—life would be so much simpler.

'Thanks—er, no I don't think I will now, Anna. I have to find Mike. Have you seen him?'

'Over there,' said Anna, pointing, and as he ran away she thankfully put the sweet she had been going to give him into her own mouth.

Miss Copewell brought a cup of tea into Mr Sage's room, and he sat there thoughtfully sipping it. Although he had dismissed Spiky, because you can't have children criticising teachers, he was nevertheless a little disturbed that Mr Smith was in the habit of giving sweets to Class 8. After a while he took up the phone and dialled Mr Browser's number.

'How are things, George? Any chance of your coming back to school soon?'

'Yes, I'm very much stronger now, and I hope to return on Monday morning.'

'Good man! Look after yourself until then.'

Mr Sage really looked pleased when he rang off, a change which had only come about because of Spiky's description of how Mr Smith was in the habit of giving out sweets. However good a teacher might be, the giving out of sweets should not be part of his duties, so Mr Sage believed—except perhaps on outings or at parties. When all the classes were back at work again, Mr Sage left his room and informed Miss Copewell that she could expect the return of Mr Browser on Monday.

'Good,' said Miss Copewell, turning the handle of her duplicating machine. Mr Sage was curious.

'What do you think of Mr Smith?' he asked her.

'Oh, I've nothing against him,' said Miss Copewell carefully. 'He doesn't mix with the other teachers, but that's his own business. But the school has been so quiet since he came here.'

'I suppose that's no bad thing,' observed the

Headmaster.

'It doesn't seem natural to me,' declared Miss Copewell. 'Not that it's any of my business, of course.'

'Of course,' said Mr Sage, and recalled how often she had said this when he had taken her good advice. He went straight to Class 8's room. He was met with silence, as the class worked away at some sums with very large numbers in them. Without thinking, Mr Sage looked at Spiky, who was counting on his fingers, a sad expression on his face.

'All busy, I see, Mr Smith,' said the Headmaster.

'Yes, Mr Sage—they're becoming used to my methods, I think.'

Mr Sage ignored this answer, because it didn't fit in with what he had to say.

'I've just been on the phone to Mr Browser, and he intends to come back to school on Monday,' he said.

Mr Smith frowned, and then gave Michael Fairlie and Spiky Jackson a threatening look, for they had overheard Mr Sage's words.

'I'm surprised to hear that,' he said. 'Are you quite sure? After an illness like that I would have expected Mr Browser to take a little more time off in order to recover properly.'

'He sounded fit enough to me,' declared Mr Sage,

shrugging his shoulders. 'He was sure that he would be coming back. Maybe you'll be able to come to Chivvy Chase again one day, Mr Smith, should one of my teachers fall ill.'

Mr Smith was not listening to him. There was a wild, desperate look in his eyes which the Headmaster had never seen before.

'Perhaps I should come to school on Monday just in case Mr Browser changes his mind,' said the teacher. 'He might not feel up to it when the day comes.'

'Do so if you like,' said the Headmaster, 'but I must tell you that if George Browser says something, he usually means it. I'm sure you'll be making a wasted journey. Your pay will be sent on to you by post. Come and see me before you leave this afternoon, won't you?'

And Mr Sage left, as he usually did, when he felt there was no more to be said. Had he stayed, he would have been surprised at the effect his words had on the stand-in teacher. Mr Smith wandered around the classroom muttering, and he had lost all the calm and smoothness which had been his trademark up to then. Spiky watched him secretly. The news of Mr Browser's coming return had acted on the man like a blow on the head. He was walking about like a fly that had been swatted.

'There's something fishy about him, Mike,'

whispered Spiky. 'He just can't bear the thought of old Browser coming back.'

'Oh, forget it, Spiky,' replied Michael. 'He's probably just mad that he can't earn any more money.'

'I think he's mad that he can't feed you any more sweets!' declared Spiky bluntly, and then put his head down to work as Mr Smith approached his desk. For the rest of the day the teacher piled work upon the class, as if to protect himself against some danger; and at the end of the afternoon he collected their books and prepared to dismiss them promptly. Then Spiky put a question to him, partly out of curiosity and partly with mischievous intent.

'Please, Mr Smith, are we saying goodbye to you this afternoon?'

The teacher frowned, as if ready to tell Spiky off; but suddenly the frown disappeared and he smiled his old smile.

'Why do you ask?'

'Isn't Mr Browser coming back on Monday, sir?'

'I wouldn't count on it, if I were you,' replied Mr Smith. 'Now you can lead on.'

He watched the class file out, then hastily packed his briefcase and made off to Mr Sage's room.

'Thank you for all the work you've done,' said Mr Sage politely. 'I have your address and will get in touch with you if you're needed again.'

'Which I probably will be on Monday,' said Mr Smith, and then bit his lip as though he wished he'd never said it.

'I doubt it,' said Mr Sage. 'George Browser is quite a tough customer.'

They parted on friendly terms, and Mr Smith went straight to the shop in Chase Road. He greeted Mrs Beacon briefly, then shut himself once more in his flat in order to communicate with his masters. After a while he came running downstairs and called Mrs Beacon into the room behind the shop.

'I'm sorry to have to tell you, Mrs Beacon, that I shan't be needing you any longer,' he told her. 'I shall be leaving shortly, and I shall be closing the shop down.'

'But you can't do that!' protested Mrs Beacon. 'You have to give me at least one week's notice—'

'I'm afraid circumstances don't allow that,' said Mr Smith, shaking his head. 'I shall, of course, pay you well before you leave—in fact, I'll give you a month's extra pay. I'm very sorry, but there's nothing else I can do.'

He went to the till and handed her a wad of five pound notes. She counted them, and began to look a little less displeased.

'I hope that will satisfy you,' he said, and brought her coat. 'Goodbye, Mrs Beacon, and thank you for your services,' he said, and in no time she was walking home, wondering what to do with the money. Mr Smith changed the OPEN sign on the door to CLOSED, and collected up all the Mind Bogglers, Taste Bud Ticklers, Lip Smackers and Telly Mates and put them in a large box in his bedroom. Then he opened the telephone directory and hunted for the name George Browser in it. When he had found it, he jotted Mr Browser's number down on a piece of paper and put it in his wallet. Once that was done, he paced up and down for a while, thinking hard.

Spiky Jackson made a point of walking home with Michael Fairlie and Selwyn Jordan. He was determined on a last effort to make them realise that something was odd about Mr Smith and his sweets.

'You heard Mr Sage say that Mr Browser is coming back on Monday, Mike, didn't you?' he pleaded.

'Yes, I heard that,' said Michael, 'and I don't know that I'm pleased about it. We're getting on very well with Mr Smith—and I like his sweets.'

'So do I,' added Selwyn.

'But there's no life at school any more!' protested Spiky. 'He's treating you like machines—and I bet his sweets have something in them to keep you all quiet. You're more like puppets than children!'

'That's what you think, Spiky. Mr Smith says

we'll have a better chance of getting jobs when we grow up,' said Selwyn, 'and I don't miss games and P.E. and art all that much.'

'You never did!' declared Spiky irritably. 'But I miss them, and surely you do, Mike?'

'I used to like them,' admitted Michael.

'Then think—why aren't you missing them any more?' Spiky put to him.

'I suppose it's because this new teacher keeps us all so busy,' replied Michael doubtfully.

'Browser kept you busy,' said Spiky. 'No, it's because his so-called sweets are sending your minds to sleep. Mind Bogglers indeed! They ought to be called Mind—Mind Shrinkers!'

'There could be something in it,' said Selwyn Jordan.

'Of course there's something in it. And who knows what he's up to now? When Sage said Mr Browser was coming back on Monday, Smith could hardly hide his anger. He's been mad about it ever since—and he even told Mr Sage that he doubted whether Browser would be back on Monday after all.'

'Perhaps he'll miss the money,' suggested Selwyn.

'No, there's more to it than that, I'm sure,' declared Spiky. 'He doesn't want to lose control of you—why, I don't understand. Don't eat any more of those sweets, Mike, and maybe you'll soon see things the same way as I do.'

Selwyn, who had only eaten the two daily sweets provided by Mr Smith that day, and was by nature very thoughtful, was prepared to consider the idea.

'It does seem rather odd—' he admitted—but before he could say any more Michael interrupted him.

'Odd—rubbish! I like those sweets, and I'm not hanging about here any longer. I'm off to buy some more.'

He set off at a trot, and the other two followed him, Spiky despairing of Michael but still hoping to win Selwyn over. If only he had one ally in his fight against Mr Smith and his mind-shrinking sweets! As they neared the shop, Mike ran faster, and he was well ahead of them when he reached it. Instead of going inside, to their surprise he stood on the pavement staring at the door.

'It's closed!' he said as they arrived alongside him. Sure enough, the CLOSED sign hung on the door, and there was no sign of life inside the shop.

'Closed at this time—that's curious,' said Selwyn. Mike said nothing, but he had a pained look on his face, and with his hands protecting his eyes from the light he kept staring in through the shop window.

'Come on, Mike, there's no point in waiting,' said

Spiky, who was pleased the shop was shut. 'If you don't eat any more sweets, you may come to your senses.'

'The sweets have disappeared—the Mind Bogglers and the others. Somebody must have taken them away,' said Mike.

'I told you something odd is going on,' said Spiky. 'Maybe the police have closed the shop down.'

'Why should they?' grumbled Michael. 'I shall be back tomorrow morning. Maybe he's only closed the shop because he's gone out somewhere.'

'Maybe,' said Spiky. 'But I bet it's not open tomorrow.'

'Come with me, and we'll see,' said Mike.

'I'll come too,' said Selwyn, and they arranged to meet again at ten o'clock the next day.

When they arrived once again outside the sweetshop, it was as closed and lifeless as it had been on the day before.

'Perhaps the shop wasn't making enough money for him,' said Michael.

'That's hard to believe,' said Spiky. 'Not with all these kids coming for sweets.'

Every few minutes children came to the door of the shop. Some couldn't believe that it was closed, and in spite of the notice they banged on the door and pushed against it—but all in vain. Some of the smaller ones burst into tears because they couldn't have any Mind Bogglers.

'Look at that,' Spiky told Selwyn and Michael. 'I tell you there's something funny about those sweets. Those kids are behaving as if they couldn't exist without them.'

As Michael and Selwyn hadn't eaten any of the sweets for more than twelve hours, they were a little more inclined to listen to Spiky.

'They are making a big fuss,' agreed Selwyn, and he went up to two small boys of about six years old, who were staring tearfully in at the shop window.

'Cheer up, you two,' he told them. 'There are other sweetshops about.'

'But not selling the same sweets,' answered the bigger of the two. 'We like the Mind Bogglers and Lip Smackers best. They're better than any of the sweets you can buy in other shops.'

'Well, you won't be buying any more,' Spiky told them. 'You'd better make do with what you can get somewhere else.'

The two boys gave a last sad look at the shop, then turned away.

'There you are,' said Spiky to his friends, 'now that you haven't been eating those rotten sweets for a while, you're beginning to see that I'm right.'

'I don't know about that,' said Michael.

'Maybe,' admitted Selwyn.

'Now I'm going to see old Browser, to make sure he's coming back on Monday,' went on Spiky. 'I'm going to tell him about the sweets, too. Are you coming?'

As they had nothing else of importance to do, now that their mission for sweets had proved in vain, they agreed, not very enthusiastically.

'I bet he'll be out,' said Michael.

As they set off for Mr Browser's road, that

gentleman was carrying his electric lawnmower to his front garden, as during his illness the grass had grown to a length much too long for Mrs Browser. That lady had gone to visit her mother, leaving Mr Browser with strict instructions not to do too much.

'Only cut the front lawn today,' she said. 'You can do the back tomorrow.'

Mr Browser had just switched on the power for the mower when the phone rang.

'Hello, Mr Browser. This is Mr Smith speaking—I took over your class in your absence.'

'Yes, of course,' said Mr Browser. 'I hope Class 8 gave you a reasonable time. They're a lively bunch.'

There was a slight silence before Mr Smith answered him, as though he hadn't understood Mr Browser's meaning.

'All went very well,' he said. 'We have done considerable work.'

'So I've heard,' said Mr Browser, smiling as he thought of Spiky's description of the work. 'Won't do them any harm, I'm sure. I'll carry on the good work on Monday.'

'Ah—Monday,' said Mr Smith. 'That's what I wanted to ring you about. I believe you told Mr Sage you would be coming back on Monday.'

'That's right.'

'Well, I have a message for you. I spoke to Mr Sage, and he's agreed that I should stay with the class on Monday. I have so much work to go over with them, that he agreed that you could put off your return until Tuesday. I'm sure that you won't mind that, will you?'

'Well—er,' stammered Mr Browser in surprise.

'He told me to tell you about it, because he's away this weekend. He would have told you himself, had he been here.'

It was Mr Browser's turn to be silent for a little thought. 'It's very unusual,' he said, playing for time.

'I can assure you it's correct,' Mr Smith told him. 'Just you relax and leave them to me until Tuesday. Agreed?'

Mr Smith appeared to be so keen that Mr Browser hadn't the heart to say no to him. Maybe Spiky Jackson wouldn't be pleased, but it was, after all, only for one day, and it was a pleasant surprise to come across a supply teacher who wanted more of Class 8.

'Agreed,' he said. 'I'll phone Mr Sage about it some time.'

'Oh, you don't need to do that,' said Mr Smith. 'I'll phone him to confirm that I'll be there on Monday. So pleased to hear that you are better. Goodbye, Mr Browser.'

Mr Browser put the receiver down after staring at it as though he couldn't believe in the sounds that had come out of it, then, shaking his head, he went thoughtfully to mow the lawn. Ten minutes later Spiky, Michael and Selwyn came to his front gate, delighted to see that they would be saved the trouble of knocking and perhaps having to persuade Mrs Browser to let them see her husband.

'Hello, Mr Browser!'

Life is full of surprises, thought Mr Browser, as he switched off the mower.

'Hello, you three. Going for a walk?'

'We came to see you, Mr Browser,' said Spiky.

'An unexpected pleasure,' said Mr Browser, coming to the gate. 'Having trouble with some work, are you?'

'No, it's not that, Mr Browser,' replied Spiky. 'We've come partly to make sure that you're going to be back in school on Monday. We heard Mr Sage say you would be, but Mr Smith didn't seem to be sure.'

'I was going to come back,' said Mr Browser, 'but now I'm waiting until Tuesday. Mr Sage has said that Mr Smith has plenty of work to finish off with the class.'

Spiky turned to his friends.

'There you are, Mike,' he said. 'I told you Smith is up to something. You heard Mr Sage say that Mr Browser should be back on Monday, didn't you?'

'Yes, I did,' agreed Michael.

'What do you mean by saying Mr Smith is up to something?' asked Mr Browser.

'He's been feeding the class some special sweets, Mr Browser. Mind Bogglers, Lip Smackers, Taste Bud Ticklers and Telly Mates—and Class 8 is like a flock of sheep. They do just as he tells them, and are happy only doing boring sums with big numbers in them. They don't want to do anything which makes them think for themselves, Mr Browser. He was mad when he heard you were coming back on Monday, and now he's told you not to come back. I think he's talked Mr Sage into letting him stay on, and who knows what he has planned for Class 8! These two are still under his power a bit, Mr Browser, and if I hadn't been on holiday, I would be too!'

Spiky had never made such a long speech in his life before, and Mr Browser turned seriously to Mike and Selwyn.

'Well, you two, what have you to say to all this?' he asked.

The two in question looked as though their minds were being split in two.

'We don't really know, Mr Browser,' replied Michael. 'We've been getting on all right with Mr Smith, until Spiky—er, Simon—started talking to us today. The sweets tasted very good.'

'Yes, I don't see how sweets could do any harm,' said Selwyn. 'Not sweets like that.'

'There you are, Mr Browser,' said Spiky. 'They don't care what happens as long as they can have their sweets.'

'I have a question for you, Michael and Selwyn,' said Mr Browser. 'Which teacher would you prefer to have on Monday, Mr Smith or me?'

'Oh, we'd rather have you, Mr Browser—if we could still have the sweets,' replied Michael.

'Yes, that would be ideal, Mr Browser,' added Selwyn politely. 'You and the sweets would be fine.'

'Is that so?' said Mr Browser quietly. 'Well, I'm afraid you won't ever find me giving out sweets in class, unless it's during the Christmas Party. This is all very interesting, Simon, and I may go to the shop and have a word with Mr Smith. Now I'd better get on with mowing my lawn.'

'Thank you, Mr Browser,' said Spiky, and the boys walked away.

Mr Browser pushed his lawnmower up and down a couple of times, but as soon as the boys were out of sight he switched off the power and went indoors to phone Mr Sage. After a while he gave up, for Mr Sage was not there, which tended to confirm what Mr Smith had said. Mr Browser finished mowing the lawn, still thinking about Spiky's story and remembering how keen Michael and Selwyn undoubtedly were about the sweets.

Perhaps it was the thought that they would only prefer him to Mr Smith as a teacher if they could have the sweets as well, which hurt his pride and made him decide to investigate further. Maybe, he thought, it would be a good idea if he bought a few of those strange sweets and kept them as evidence in case of trouble. He knew his wife would not be back for at least another hour, and it was only a quarter of an hour's walk to the shop, so he didn't bother to leave a message.

On his way to the shop he met Mrs Beacon, and couldn't resist stopping to ask her one or two questions.

'What do you think of the new owner, Mrs Beacon?' It was an unfortunate question, but then he didn't know that she had been dismissed.

'Not much, Mr Browser, not much!' she replied, sniffing. 'He's dismissed me, and I understand he's going to close the shop. Why he started the business I can't understand.'

'He sold some unusual sweets,' said Mr Browser. 'The children in my class seem to be hooked on them.'

'Cheap stuff,' declared Mrs Beacon, 'but the children did like them.'

'Where did he obtain them, I wonder?' asked Mr Browser.

'Nobody delivered them,' said Mrs Beacon. 'He must have brought them with him. They aren't made by any of the big manufacturers.'

'Do you know where he came from himself?'

'He never mentioned it, but he really was an odd fish. Yes, fish is the right word. Sort of slimy, he was. Had no friends, and spent all his time shut in the flat above the shop. In a way I'm pleased to be away from him, though he did pay me well.'

Mr Browser thanked her and went on his way. Like the boys, he was disappointed to find the CLOSED notice on the door of the shop. He banged on the door and waited. Secretly, Mr Smith looked down from an upstairs window to see who was knocking. When he saw that it was Mr Browser, he smiled at his good fortune, and hastened down the stairs to open the door.

'Mr Browser! Do come in, please.'

'I'm surprised to find the shop closed,' said Mr Browser.

'Yes—I'm making some slight alterations. Please come up to my flat.'

'I only came to see if I could buy some of those sweets the children are so keen about,' said Mr Browser. 'Mind Bogglers, or something. Very popular, they are.'

'Yes, indeed,' replied Mr Smith. 'Unfortunately I've run out of them at the moment. Why not have another of the kind I gave you before?'

Mr Smith looked so keen to go and get one, and so pleased with himself for having had the idea, that Mr Browser became uneasy.

'No, no—please don't bother now,' he said.

Mr Smith brought out a bag from a drawer.

'No thank you,' said Mr Browser. 'I just want to tell you that I'll be coming in to school on Monday morning after all. I really am fit enough to start again—'

Mr Smith scowled at him.

'A sweet—I insist,' he said.

'No, thank you—'

'Have it your own way,' said Mr Smith, and his arm shot out towards Mr Browser.

'I insist,' repeated Mr Smith, and smiled his smoothest smile as Mr Browser sank to the floor in front of him.

Mrs Browser was a little late back from her mother's because she was delayed in a dress shop on the way home. She was pleased to see the front lawn looking neater, but puzzled because it didn't look as though the job had been completed. She wondered whether Mr Browser was now repairing her vacuum cleaner, as he had promised to do.

'George,' she called as she let herself in and closed the door. 'George—I'm back.'

Perhaps he's in the back garden, she thought. But he wasn't. He did not answer any of her calls. She shook her head, and began to prepare a meal. When it was ready and he still hadn't appeared, she became worried, and rang several friends and relations in case he had gone to visit them. She ate the meal alone, and soon became seriously alarmed. After consulting with friends and neighbours, she at last did what she had been

considering for some time. She rang the police station.

Mr Browser was officially missing.

6
Deadline Monday Morning

For the children of Class 8 the weekend passed like any normal weekend—except that from time to time hopeful customers would appear outside Mr Smith's shop. Their hopes were dashed, for the shop remained closed and lifeless all the time. The news of Mr Browser's disappearance did not spread to the children, for the police and Mrs Browser were first of all checking the possibility that he had gone off on his own accord to visit relatives or friends.

On Sunday Mr Sage was contacted, and the police asked him if Mr Browser had been under any extra strain at school. Mr Sage said no—taking Class 8 every day was not like a holiday, but Mr Browser managed very well. Of course, a nasty attack of 'flu could make people feel very low, and maybe that had affected him. The police said they'd thought of that, and Mr Sage said that he had been expecting Mr Browser back on Monday morning.

By Sunday evening Mrs Browser was desperate, and told so many people that the news spread to Anna Cardwell, whose aunt lived a few doors away from the Browsers. Anna arrived at school early on

Monday morning, and wasted no time in telling as many of Class 8 as she could about Mr Browser. Quick checks were made, and Selwyn reported that Mr Browser's car was not to be seen in the school car park.

'He does walk to school sometimes,' said Anna, 'but I haven't seen him myself.'

'If he doesn't turn up, we shan't have a teacher,' said Michael Fairlie. 'Old Sage told Smith that Mr Browser would be back.'

'I've a feeling we shall have a teacher,' said Spiky mysteriously. The class hurried into school when the bell went, all much more eager than usual on a Monday morning.

'You're right, Spiky!' whispered Michael as they reached the door of Classroom 8.

Inside, seated at Mr Browser's desk and smiling broadly, was Mr Smith. Two scaring thoughts passed through Spiky's mind as he went to his place. Firstly—did Mr Smith know that Mr Browser would be missing? Secondly, and much the more scaring of the two—had Mr Smith something to do with Mr Browser's absence?

'Good morning, Class 8,' said Mr Smith when they were all seated. 'I'm pleased to say that I am with you still.'

'Where's Mr Browser?' called out Anna boldly—she hadn't eaten a Mind Boggler all weekend.

'He's not well enough to come to school yet,' replied Mr Smith.

'He's missing!' said Selwyn loudly, and Mr Smith frowned.

'That's enough,' he said. 'We have much to do today. First of all the usual helpers can give out the sweets.'

'Don't eat one!' Spiky warned Anna as she went out to collect the sweets for her group. 'I think I know where Browser could be—and I think Smith knows too!'

Most of the class gratefully popped the sweets into their mouths, but Anna, Michael, Selwyn and Spiky hid them. Mr Smith then rushed through the calling of the register, and the class prepared for the expected list of words for spelling. It did not come. Mr Smith stood up.

'Pay attention, everyone,' he said. 'I know that some of you have missed your P.E. and games lessons since I have been teaching you, so this morning I want to put that right. As you haven't had much exercise lately, we'll start off with a gentle walk, with perhaps a little jogging now and again. If you have your P.E. shoes with you, put them on, but if not, don't worry. As soon as you are ready, line up at the door.'

'But—' objected Michael, 'we have to go to Assembly first on Monday mornings.'

Mr Smith's smile vanished.

'You will do as I say,' he replied, 'and without any delay.'

'He's up to something,' whispered Spiky, hanging back with Anna, Michael and Selwyn as the rest of the class moved happily to the door, highly pleased to be doing something different. Mr Smith tapped impatiently on the desk, and glared at the four who were bringing up the rear. He looked at his watch, and hurried to the front of the line.

'Lead on!' he commanded them.

'I don't like it,' muttered Spiky. 'He's in such a hurry to get out of the classroom, whereas before he never let us go even to the hall. I bet he wants to do something with the class before Mr Browser comes back.'

'I think,' said Selwyn, his old thoughtfulness returning to him, 'that he may have stopped Mr Browser coming back to school.'

'Exactly!' agreed Spiky. 'But where can old Browser be?'

'Cor!' exclaimed Anna, surprised to have been hit by a sudden idea. 'Suppose he's locked up in the sweetshop?'

'You could be right,' said Spiky.

'But where's Smith going to take the class?' asked Michael.

'We don't know, yet,' admitted Spiky, 'but I'm

pretty sure it won't do them any good, or why would he be so secretive about it? We ought to warn Mr Sage.'

'We can't all do that,' suggested Selwyn. 'Four of us would be missed. Michael and I will go with the class to see what's going on, and you and Anna can stay behind and tell Mr Sage what's happened. Maybe one boy and one girl won't be missed so quickly.'

'Good idea,' agreed Spiky as the class followed Mr Smith along the downstairs corridor, Mr Smith urging them on as if he feared someone else might pass by and notice them. 'Be ready, Anna—drop back a little, and Mike and Selwyn stay at the back of the class, so that we won't be missed. The others would tell him, for sure!'

As the little victims of the Mind Bogglers followed Mr Smith out of a side door which led into the playground, Anna and Spiky kept straight on until they arrived at Mr Sage's room. Spiky banged so hard on his door that the Headmaster thought that someone important must be outside.

'Come in, please!' he called out, and rose to his feet in order to greet the important person. To his surprise, two children burst into the room.

'Mr Sage—' began Spiky, but the Headmaster cut him short.

'Close the door behind you, Simon, and calm

down, please. You're not in the playground now!'

'But the rest of the class are!' Spiky dared to say as Anna quickly closed the door, and they both stood on the little Persian carpet before Mr Sage's desk and tried to look obedient. Mr Sage sat down again and was about to ask Spiky to explain his presence, when Anna could keep quiet no longer.

'Please, Mr Sage, we think we know where Mr Browser is!'

'And,' Spiky joined in, 'Mr Smith has taken the class out somewhere, before Assembly, Mr Sage!'

'And we think it's Mr Smith who has made Mr

Browser go missing!' added Anna. She was so excited that without realising it she walked up to Mr Sage's desk and leaned right over it, she was so determined to make him understand. Mr Sage was so surprised by what he had heard that he quite forgot to tell her off.

'Calm down,' he said again, 'and explain exactly what you mean. Simon, you speak first.'

He pressed the buzzer which told Miss Copewell, his secretary, to come in at once.

'I think Mr Smith has planned that Mr Browser couldn't come to school—' began Spiky, and launched into a full description of all that had happened.

'Yes, Mr Sage?' Miss Copewell poked her head round the door.

'Just check up where Class 8 is, Miss Copewell, please. These children say that Mr Smith has taken them outside. Maybe they're in the playground.'

'They won't be, by now,' said Anna, and Mr Sage frowned at her. Miss Copewell's head disappeared, and Spiky brought his story up to date. Just as he had finished, Miss Copewell appeared again.

'They're nowhere in sight, Mr Sage,' she said. 'Some of Mr Caracco's class said they saw them go out of the school grounds by the car park entrance.'

'Before Assembly!' muttered Mr Sage. 'It's certainly rather odd.'

'We ought to go at once to the shop,' said Anna, 'just to make sure Mr Browser isn't there.'

'We can't go and break into the shop,' said the Headmaster. 'But I certainly didn't know that Mr Browser had been told not to come back to school today,' he added, and stood there frowning.

'Take these children into the office, Miss Copewell,' he ordered. 'I want to make a phone call.'

Anna and Spiky waited anxiously in the office. Was Mr Sage going to take action? Miss Copewell went on with her work as if nothing had happened. Then Mr Sage came into the room.

'I've rung the Education Office,' he said, 'and they are checking with the college where Mr Smith said he trained to be a teacher. As soon as they ring back, I shall know what to do.'

'But they might be ages,' protested Anna. 'Poor Mr Browser—'

'Quiet, Anna,' said Mr Sage, and they had to spend more minutes waiting.

'Please send a message round to say that Assembly has to be postponed,' Mr Sage told Miss Copewell. 'I can't afford to go far from the telephone at the moment.'

Miss Copewell obeyed—and before she came back the phone rang. Mr Sage ran into his room to take the call. He was there for what seemed to Spiky and Anna a very long time, and Miss Copewell had been back for some minutes before he reappeared.

'The college said they'd never heard of him,' said Mr Sage. 'No one by the name of Sebastian Smith has ever attended there. So I've rung the police, and they want me to go to the shop at once and meet them there.'

'May we come too?' asked Anna, expecting to be refused. Mr Sage had forgotten all about the children, but his reply surprised her.

'As a matter of fact you can,' he replied. 'You may be able to help the police. There's no time to waste—come to my car at once!'

They had never seen Mr Sage move so fast, and they were hard put to it to keep up with him as he ran to the car park.

'Into the back seat!' he ordered them, and revved up the engine of his 1800 CC car, which was surprised to be started so suddenly at that time of day. In five minutes they were outside the sweet-shop, parked behind a police car which had just arrived. Two policemen jumped out of the car to meet them.

'The place is deserted,' said one of them. 'No windows are open, back or front, and the curtains are all drawn in the upstairs flat. Why do you think your teacher might be in there, you children?'

'I think he went to see Mr Smith,' said Spiky,

'perhaps to tell him that he was going to come back to school today after all—and Mr Smith kept him there.'

'Sounds most unlikely,' said one of the policemen. 'I suppose we could break down the door and force an entry on the grounds of suspicious circumstances.'

'Suspecting that a missing person might be inside,' said the other policeman.

'It might become a case of a missing class as well as a missing person,' said Mr Sage.

'Let's go,' said the first policeman, and together they put their shoulders to the door and forced it open.

'Stay in the car!' Mr Sage ordered Spiky and Anna, and much as they hated it they had to obey him. He rushed after the policemen, and to Anna and Spiky it seemed like ages before anything happened. Then Mr Sage came running out of the shop.

'The policemen say you can come inside!' he called to them. 'Hurry up!'

Spiky didn't stop to grumble about the unjust way children are treated—first told to stay in the car and then to hurry up into the shop—he just fell out of the car and raced into the shop, Anna close behind him.

'Upstairs room!' called out Mr Sage. Spiky could

hear voices in the back room, and climbed the stairs two at a time and dashed along the corridor. A policeman stood at the door, but Spiky slipped past him.

'Mr Browser!' he cried, and stopped to stare at his teacher, who was sitting in an old armchair, with a scarf and a rope lying on the floor at his side. He wasn't wearing a tie, and he looked tired and worried.

'Mr Browser!' said Anna. 'We thought you'd be here. We told you, Mr Sage, didn't we! Are you all right, Mr Browser?'

'Yes, thank you, Anna,' replied Mr Browser. 'I'm very glad you've all come. My arms and legs are a bit stiff, where he tied me up, and I could do with a bite to eat, but I'll soon be fine. I refused to eat another of his wretched sweets, so he had to tie me up.'

'There's no time to waste,' said one of the policemen. 'Tell us exactly what has happened to the class. It could be that they are in danger. Your Mr Smith appears to be a very strange man.'

Spiky was looking round the room, his eyes opened wide. Along one of the walls was a strange machine—some kind of computer, perhaps, yet different from any computer he had ever seen.

'Where is the class, Simon?' asked Mr Browser.

'We don't know, Mr Browser. But we sent two

spies along with them—Selwyn and Michael, and unless he sees them they will try and come back with news of the class.'

'Very good,' said Mr Browser.

'He's taken them for a walk somewhere,' Anna told the policeman, 'But we don't know where.'

'You'd better go back to school,' said Mr Browser, 'and I'll go home, if you don't mind. I expect my wife will be worrying about me.'

'Has been for days,' said the policeman. 'We'll send a car to take you home.'

They all returned to the cars. Mr Browser came blinking into the sunshine after his captivity. Another police car drew up so that he could be taken home, and the first car led the way back to Chivvy Chase School, followed by Mr Sage, Spiky and Anna.

As they reached the car park, Michael and Selwyn came running towards them, breaking the school rule by entering the car park on foot. Mr Sage didn't think about that. He flung open the door of his car.

'Where are the rest of the class?' he demanded.

'We know, Mr Sage, we know!' cried Selwyn, waving his arms in the air like a runner who has just won a race.

'Well, where are they, lad?' asked one of the policemen, who had jumped out of his car.

'They are inside the old sandpit on the other side of the brook,' said Michael. 'That is, they were when we ran away.'

'What were they doing?' asked Mr Sage.

'They were being asked questions by Mr Smith,' said Selwyn, 'and they were all answering the questions together, like—puppets. And rays of light were coming down into the sandpit, and it seemed to be awfully hot in there. We watched from behind a tree, and then we ran.'

'Did you hear anything?' asked the policeman.

'I heard Mr Smith tell them to sit quite still and obey him absolutely, because now they were all in the power of the Mind Shrinkers!' answered Selwyn.

'Mind Shrinkers! The man must be mad,' declared the policeman. 'We must get to the sandpit at once!'

'I'm coming too!' cried Mr Sage. 'You four, lead into school—'

'No—we can't have these children loose and spreading rumours about what they've seen,' the policeman told him. 'Bring them with you—but keep a close watch on them. We'll find out the truth about all this in a few minutes. If they've been spinning us a yarn—'

'Oh, do hurry up!' pleaded Selwyn. 'If we're too late, who knows what the Mind Shrinkers will do to them!'

'Mind Shrinkers!' muttered the policeman—but he sprang back into his car and they all set off for the sandpit.

7
The Mind Shrinkers' Mental Test

When Anna and Spiky left them, Mike and Selwyn walked on at the rear of the class, and no one else appeared to have noticed that two members of the class had gone astray. Certainly Mr Smith didn't; he was striding out in the front of the line, sure that the Mind Bogglers he had given out would make the children obey him absolutely.

He took them out of a side door into the playground, and crossed it at a point where the group was unlikely to be seen. A narrow path with high fences on either side took them past the back gardens of two houses and out on the pavement of a quiet side street.

'This way!' he commanded, took a brief look round to see that they were following him, and set off at a swift pace down the road. The further he went the more impatient he became. He crossed a main road at a pedestrian crossing, and didn't even turn round to see if all the class had reached the other side safely. They did, following him much more neatly than a flock of sheep.

'He's not just walking,' whispered Selwyn to Mike. 'He's taking them somewhere special—and he can't get there quickly enough!'

Mr Smith did turn round at last, and called on the class to change from walking to running as they started up a long road which crossed a brook. It led them towards open fields.

'Why's he taking them this way?' asked Mike. 'There are only a few fields—'

'And the old sandpit,' Selwyn reminded him. 'A good place to hide.'

They had no more breath for talking. Soon they were at the end of the road and crossing the fields—in the direction of the sandpit.

'Looks as though you were right,' said Mike, panting.

They descended into the sandpit, which had been deserted years before after most of the sand had been removed. Mr Smith was leading the class in the direction of a building which stood to one side of the pit. This had once been the office of the company which had owned the sandpit. Most of its roof was off, which made it ideal for Mr Smith's purpose, but the walls were standing. Most of the windows were missing. Mr Smith led the class into the building through the space where the door had once been. Mike and Selwyn brought up the rear, and stood just inside the doorway.

'Sit down,' Mr Smith ordered the class, and went into a little room which still had a roof over it. He came back almost immediately with a sheaf of papers in his hand, and started to give one out to each child—and a pencil with it if necessary. He then returned to the little room, and this time came out with a small box, seemingly made of white plastic material, which was dotted along its side with switches. On top of it Mike and Selwyn could just make out a number of knobs, which reminded Selwyn of a typewriter. Michael afterwards compared it to a musical instrument, and said that he expected Mr Smith to start pressing them in order to play it.

What actually happened next was so extraordinary that the two boys were in danger of forgetting that they were trying to keep themselves apart from the rest of the class. Mr Smith flicked over a switch, watched the box carefully and flicked another one. Suddenly the knobs on the top of the box were hit by yellow rays—at first Selwyn thought it was lightning—and they went up and down as though some invisible musician were playing an instrument. Mr Smith had paper and pencil with him, and while the knobs were moving he was writing very quickly. Just as suddenly the rays ceased and the knobs were still. Mr Smith turned to the class.

'The first question to be answered is this,' he said to them. 'Do you believe that Mind Bogglers are the

best sweets you have ever eaten?'

The class wrote their answers.

'How many answered "yes"—please show,' asked Mr Smith.

Every member of the class—except for Selwyn and Mike, who had hidden themselves on the outside of the doorway—put up his or her hand.

'Good,' said Mr Smith, and pressed the switches again. The rays came down on the knobs, and he wrote down their message.

'Question two,' he announced. 'Who do you think is the best teacher you have ever had?'

The class wrote their answers.

'And what did you put, Jason?' asked Mr Smith hopefully.

'Mr Smith,' replied Jason, and Mr Smith's smile seemed to make his glasses twinkle.

'How many of you agree with Jason?' he asked.

Every member of the class put up a hand, and Mr Smith's smile became even broader. 'Next question,' he said, and worked the switches again. 'Now answer this,' he asked them when the rays had done their work. 'Will you promise to do everything he tells you?'

Michael and Selwyn could see the hands of the class going up again as Mr Smith asked them for their replies, and a look of pure triumph came on his face as he saw that they were all agreed. He flicked the switches to receive the next question. Michael beckoned to Selwyn, and they crept away from the door to stand outside the building.

'They're being brainwashed,' Selwyn whispered to Michael. 'He must be in contact with some outside power, or else he's faking the whole thing.'

'He couldn't fake those rays,' declared Michael, and, fascinated, they hesitated for a moment to listen.

'And now the next question,' Mr Smith was saying. 'Do you promise to eat your sweets daily, and to obey Mr Smith and the Mind Shrinkers absolutely when they arrive on Earth?'

'Now we know!' whispered Selwyn. 'He's preparing them to become slaves of the Mind Shrinkers! We'd better get back to school as fast as we can and warn somebody. Who knows what that creature means to do with them!'

First of all they tip-toed away from the building, then ran up the path from the sandpit and down the road which led back in the direction of Chivvy Chase School. Breathlessly they met up with Anna, Spiky, Mr Sage and the policemen, and gasped out some of their story. Mr Sage drove fast with them in the direction of the pit, but he couldn't keep up with the police car, which soon disappeared ahead of them. They could hear its siren wailing in the distance, and as Mr Sage reached the beginning of the disused track which led off the road, they caught a glimpse of it as it turned down the path to the pit.

The siren went on wailing, and as they reached the edge of the pit they could see the policemen getting out of the car. Mr Smith's waxlike face appeared for a second at the doorway, but as soon as he saw the police car he went inside again. The policemen were advancing towards the door, and Mr Sage was carefully driving along the bumpy path, when the sky was lit up by a brilliant flash.

The policemen staggered to the ground, and a small flame and a wisp of smoke curled up from the little room at the end of the building. Mr Sage, shocked, jammed on his brakes, and the children lurched forward.

'Look!' cried Anna. Mr Smith came out of the doorway, clutching the box they had seen him use when asking his questions. Taking a look around him, and making sure the policemen were flat on the ground, he started to run along the side of the building, away from the cars.

'After him!' said Spiky, flinging the car door open. 'Don't let him escape.'

He sprang out, followed by the other three.

'Come back!' shouted Mr Sage, but only Spiky answered.

'Look after the other children, Mr Sage!' he

called back.

Mr Smith disappeared round the corner of the building, and soon the four children followed. There was nothing Mr Sage could do but make his way to the policemen, who were groaning as they lay on the ground.

'What about the class?' Anna called to Spiky as they ran.

'We'll have to leave them to Mr Sage,' said Spiky. 'We're the only ones who can see where Smith goes. He's running towards some trees. Come on!'

Mr Smith disappeared over the top of the sandpit as the four were scrambling up the small cliff which formed the edge of it. Once up at the top they caught a glimpse of him in the distance. He couldn't run at full speed because of the box he was holding. That box must be very special, thought Spiky, or he'd throw it away and move faster.

They were running over bumpy ground covered with long, coarse grass, and ahead of them was a clump of trees. Mr Smith was making for these—and was a hundred metres ahead of them as he disappeared amidst them. They slowed down as they reached the trees, but Spiky urged them on.

'There aren't many trees,' he said. 'He can't easily hide there.'

They moved carefully from tree to tree, hoping not to come upon Mr Smith suddenly. A grassy field soon came into sight, with one tree standing on it, a tree which looked as if it had been punished for leaving the others by being struck by lightning. High up on the thick trunk were branches reaching out like fingers, one of them split open by the force of the lightning flash.

Spiky was the first to see Mr Smith running across the grass to the tree, and he held out his arms to make sure the others stopped. From the cover of the trees they watched as Mr Smith threw the box he was holding high in the air, in the direction of the lower branches of the tree. They saw it rise above the top of the tree trunk, then fall—and disappear inside the tree. As soon as the box had gone, Mr Smith rushed towards the trunk, sprang up against it and managed to grab the lowest branch. He clambered to the top of the trunk, and then, just like the box, lowered himself into the tree and disappeared!

'It's a hollow tree!' whispered Anna. 'Why has he gone in there?'

'Let's go and find out,' suggested Spiky, but Selwyn shook his head.

'I wouldn't try it, for two reasons,' he said. 'Firstly, none of us could reach the lowest branch, and the trunk's too large for us to put our arms round it and pull ourselves up it. Secondly, by going into that tree he's made himself a prisoner. We should go back to the pit and tell Mr Sage and the policemen where he is.'

'You're right,' said Michael. 'But shouldn't one of us stay here in case he climbs out before they come?'

'I don't suppose he'll climb out before dark,' said Selwyn, 'but you can stay if you like. Whatever you do, don't let yourself be seen!'

'I won't,' promised Michael, and sat down behind a tree as the other three hurried away. He kept his eyes on the hollow tree all the time, but after a while became bored with his task. If Mr Smith had jumped inside the tree, why should he want to escape from it so soon, he reasoned. No doubt Selwyn was right, and when darkness fell something might happen, but not before, unless when the police returned they decided to drag him out, or perhaps smoke him out.

While Michael was busy with these thoughts, he was surprised to see a ray of what seemed like lightning shoot down to the tree. The sky, as far as he could see from under the trees, was completely blue—so he decided that it must have been a ray of light which had deceived him. But then another ray came, and more and more—and all of them directed down inside the tree. Michael stood up and retreated a little behind another tree a little distance away.

The rays continued for a while, and he was becoming used to them, when something even stranger happened. Instead of shooting downwards, the rays began to flow upwards from inside the tree. They were whiter than the downward ones, and more of them shot up together, rising high into the sky until they disappeared. At any moment Michael expected to see the tree burst into flames, but it didn't, and in what he thought to be about five minutes, but was probably less, the rays ceased and the tree stood peacefully, leaving Michael to wonder whether he had imagined what he thought he had seen.

He was still wondering when he heard the sound of footsteps coming through the trees, at first quickly and quite noisily, and then much more quietly.

'Mike!' came Spiky's voice. 'Are you all right?'

'Of course,' replied Michael. Spiky appeared, and with him Anna, Mr Sage and the two policemen.

'What's happened to the class?' asked Michael.

'Mr Browser came back and took them all to school,' said Anna. 'As soon as he'd seen Mrs Browser he made straight for the sandpit. Miss Copewell told him where Selwyn and you had come from.'

'And has anything happened here, boy?' asked one of the policemen impatiently. Michael thought

about the rays, and decided against telling about them yet.

'Mr Smith must still be inside that tree,' he told them, pointing to the hollow tree.

'So—that's the tree,' said the policeman. 'If he's dropped to ground level, he won't find it easy to escape from there.'

'That we can't tell,' said the other policeman. 'Do you boys know anything about this tree?'

They shook their heads.

'Its branches are too high for us to be able to climb it,' said Spiky.

'That's true. There's only one way to see what's going on in there—we'll have to climb it ourselves,' said the first policeman. 'Give me a leg up, and I'll take a look inside.'

They took off their caps, rolled up their sleeves and took up position beside the tree.

'Here goes!' One of them made a back for the other, who sprang from there and managed to cling on to the lowest branch. With its help he clambered up the trunk and stood looking down into the tree.

'What can you see?'

'Nothing,' he replied, and Michael stared up at him in disbelief. 'Yes, there's something,' he added. 'A few burnt clothes at the bottom, that's all. Oh yes, and a pair of horn-rimmed spectacles resting on a kind of ledge inside.

'Those are Mr Smith's,' called out Spiky.

'Come up here,' the policeman told his colleague. 'If you give me a hand, I think I can reach down and bring up the glasses. We can present them as evidence when we go back, and then maybe a thorough examination of the tree will be made.'

The second policeman, hauled up by the first, reached the top of the trunk and held on to him while he lowered himself headfirst into the tree.

'Ever seen an upside down policeman?' joked his comrade.

'Okay, coming up,' he called, and heaved himself up again.

'The glasses,' he said, and perched them for a moment on the edge of the trunk.

Mr Smith's spectacles seemed to be twinkling as they returned Michael's upward gaze. It was as though something of Mr Smith remained and was smiling down at him, just as the grin of the Cheshire Cat remained when the rest of the body had gone. Now Michael could keep silent no longer.

'Something did happen while you were away,' he called up to the policemen, and when they both came down he told them all about the mysterious râys.

8
No More Mind Bogglers

The rest of the day was as exciting as the first part of it had been. They all returned to school, where Mr Browser was sitting in front of the class staring into space while his pupils were supposed to be busy with silent reading, though in fact most of them were busy with their own thoughts, trying to work out what had been happening to them and wondering about the fate of Mr Smith.

Mr Browser was soon withdrawn from the classroom, and Miss Copewell was left to take charge of the silent reading while he and the four children chiefly mixed up in the affair were answering questions in Mr Sage's room. The questioners were policemen in plain clothes, and first of all they tried to persuade Michael that perhaps Mr Smith could have escaped from the tree while he was not looking.

'But I was watching all the time,' insisted Michael, 'and I did see the rays, I'm certain. I think the rays went to the box he was probably holding—he had it in the sandpit while he put questions to the children. And how about the machine he had in the shop! Didn't rays come down to that,

Mr Browser?'

'He was certainly communicating with someone,' said Mr Browser. 'Unfortunately I was tied up and couldn't turn my head properly to see what was going on—'

'Never mind that machine now,' said one of the questioners. 'That will be looked into in due course. Now tell us what sort of questions Mr Smith was asking the class.'

They told all they could remember about the questions, and notes were taken.

'Have any of you kept any of the sweets Mr Smith gave you?' was the next question. They shook their heads.

'All the sweets were much too tasty for us to keep them,' said Anna, and gave them the names of the different kinds of sweets.

'What do you think he was up to?' asked Mr Sage—but the questioners wanted to put all the questions themselves.

'Until we have completed our tests and examinations, we shan't be able to say,' replied one of them.

Then Mr Browser, who was still a little shaky, was sent home, and the detectives went away, keeping their opinions to themselves. At the end of the school day Spiky and Michael decided to go home past the sweetshop, though they knew there would be no chance of entering it. But they found their visit well worth while, for guarding the door of the shop were not one, but two policemen—and Spiky detected a third man with a gun crouching behind a chimney. A mysterious blue van was parked opposite the shop. They hung about for a while, and saw a small, bearded man come out of the shop, go to the van and fetch out a large wooden box, which he took back into the shop.

'They're taking it very seriously,' said Spiky. 'I reckon they know old Smith was in contact with the Mind Shrinkers, but they don't want to say so.'

'Maybe he was a Mind Shrinker himself,' said Michael, 'and that's why he could disappear.'

They were thinking about this when one of the policemen at the door called across to them.

'Move along, you boys. We don't want you hanging about here.'

'There you are,' said Spiky, as they obeyed. 'They want to keep it all secret. I bet that little man with the beard is a top scientist, come to help them try and prove where Mr Smith has gone.'

'And where he came from, perhaps,' said Michael. 'Where do you think he came from, Spiky?' he added with a worried look.

'I believe he came from somewhere secret,' said Spiky, 'and I think he's gone back there, in some form or other. And I think he was trying out a plan

to shrink all our minds so that we'd do exactly what the Mind Shrinkers wanted. When he was found out too soon, they ordered him back. I'm going to find out more from Mr Browser tomorrow.'

In fact all of Class 8 awaited the arrival of Mr Browser in the classroom the next day with more than the usual interest. There were still some, to be truthful, who were missing their daily dose of Mind Bogglers or Lip Smackers, who would not have been much upset if Mr Smith had appeared again. Anna, Michael, Selwyn and Spiky sat in dread lest this should happen.

But Mr Browser arrived with his battered old briefcase, looking pale but calm.

'Good morning, Class 8,' he said, as though he had never been away. 'I hear that you worked very well with Mr Smith, which is pleasing. However, I understand that you missed certain lessons—so this morning we shall be having an extra P.E. lesson, and an art lesson this afternoon. There is more to life than tables and spellings.'

'Hurrah!' called out Jason Little.

'Nevertheless,' went on Mr Browser, frowning, 'they are also important, in their place. And you will have to become used to going without your daily ration of sweets. I don't live in a sweetshop.'

There were one or two groans at this.

'However,' he went on, 'as you've grown so

used—or should I say, addicted—to being given sweets, I shall make an exception today, and this morning at playtime each of you will receive one small bar of chocolate of a well-known make. That's my way of saying "thank you" for your part in rescuing me.'

The same children who had groaned now joined the others in raising a cheer for Mr Browser. When

it died down, Spiky took his chance.

'Mr Browser, do you think Mr Smith was one of the Mind Shrinkers himself?'

There were one or two laughs, but Mr Browser remained serious.

'You never ate any of his sweets, did you, Simon?'

'No, Mr Browser.'

'But you are the only one in the class who didn't?'

'That's right, Mr Browser. I was in Spain—'

'And how lucky we were that you were away,' said Mr Browser. 'Whether he was a Mind Shrinker or not, I can't be sure, but he was certainly a very odd kind of human being, and he was definitely keeping in touch with somebody somewhere. It is fascinating to think that if ever there were an invasion of Earth from outer space, it need not be done by bug-eyed monsters or little green men, but by—'

Mr Browser stopped because in the middle of his sentence Mr Sage walked into the room. He raised his eyebrows when he heard the words 'bug-eyed monsters', and he gave Mr Browser and the class one of his sternest looks.

'May I have a word, please, Mr Browser?' he asked without really asking.

'Of course, Mr Sage.'

'Now that Mr Browser has returned,' said Mr Sage, turning to the class, 'I hope that all of you settle down to normal work again. Mr Smith was a good teacher, but that, of course, is not enough. He was wrong to offer you sweets, and wrong to take you out of school without my permission.'

Surely that was the least important part of the wrongdoing, that he didn't tell Mr Sage, thought Mr Browser—but he kept his thoughts to himself.

'However,' went on Mr Sage, 'now that Mr Smith is gone, there will be no need to talk about him any more. Just forget all about his sweets and the trip to the sandpit, and live your lives as you did before. We shall probably never know where Mr Smith has gone, so there's no point in talking about him. Please continue with your work.'

Mr Sage turned to Mr Browser, who felt he had been included in the instructions to the class.

'By the way, that is the view of the police and the authorities generally,' declared Mr Sage quietly. 'They want the affair completely hushed up. It seems that Mr Smith was not a real teacher at all—all his papers were false. Fortunately he doesn't seem to have done the children any harm, in spite of his sweets. The sooner he's forgotten, the better.'

'How about the machines he was working?' asked Mr Browser, who was less willing to forget all about it. 'Do they know with whom he was in contact? The children have mentioned strange creatures called Mind Shrinkers—'

Mr Sage made a tut-tutting sound.

'The man must have been mad,' he said. 'You'd better stay healthy, George. We don't want any more supply teachers like that!'

Mr Sage smiled farewell and went to his room. Mr Browser felt pleased to be wanted, but still wondered about Mr Smith. Spiky interrupted his thoughts.

'You were just saying, Mr Browser, that invasion from space need not be by monsters. Then Mr Sage came in. What were you going to tell us?'

Mr Browser hesitated. Mr Sage had said that the matter was closed—but Mr Browser looked at the class and thought about their future, and decided to say one thing more.

'I was going to say, Simon, that if children can be persuaded to eat strange sweets by someone who might be an agent for creatures from space, why shouldn't the invasion come through T.V. aerials, or through our weather? People could be made to agree with anything the invaders wanted before the enemy ever landed on Earth. It could be that we have had a narrow escape, thanks chiefly to Spiky—er, Simon, but who knows how we can be attacked in the future? The Mind Shrinkers have failed this time—and let's hope they always do. And now I'm going to give out the chocolate, but please don't eat it until you're in the playground!'

'Three cheers for Mr Browser!' called out Jason Little, and Mr Browser somehow hoped the sound didn't reach Mr Sage's room.

All thoughts of the Mind Bogglers, Lip Smackers, Taste Bud Ticklers and Telly Mates were gone like a dream, when the bell for play rang and the class burst out into the playground just like the old Class 8!

9

Mr Smith Goes to Pieces

Mr Smith had never expected to depart in the daylight, but with the children and the police on his trail he knew there was nothing for it but escape. He tossed the box into the tree and followed inside the trunk himself. There he opened the box and made final contact with the Mind Shrinkers, then prepared himself to leave. He put his horn-rimmed glasses on a ledge, piled his clothes together on the ground, and waited.

Soon the rays began to come down inside the trunk, and he felt his arms and legs beginning to melt away. The rays became more intense, and like a candle burning too fast he sank down to the ground, as the wax runs down the side of the candle and spreads out on the saucer beneath. In a few moments all that remained of Mr Smith's human appearance was a waxy collection of cells lying like jellyfish on the ground.

At once the rays changed their colour, and the cells began to move upwards, as if absorbed into the rays. In less than five minutes only the clothes and the glasses remained to show that Mr Smith had once been on Earth, and no sooner was all trace of him gone than the hollow tree was struck, it seemed, by lightning, and all that remained of the clothes was a charred mass.

The experiment of the Mind Shrinkers at Chivvy Chase was over.